Excellent '95

T5-DHB-591

The Barrier

ZONDERVAN HEARTH BOOKS

Available from your Christian Bookseller

A HEARTH ROMANCE

The Barrier

Sallie Lee Bell

ZONDERVAN
PUBLISHING HOUSE
OF THE ZONDERVAN CORPORATION | GRAND RAPIDS, MICHIGAN 49506

THE BARRIER
Copyright 1957 by
Zondervan Publishing House
Grand Rapids, Michigan

Ninth printing   1979
ISBN 0-310-20982-X
Printed in the United States of America

CHAPTER 1

MEREDITH MAINTAINED THAT IT WAS THE LORD who led her past that particular spot at that particular hour on that particular day, though skeptics smirked and friends smiled whenever she told them how she felt about what happened that day.

Friends who knew the end of the story but who lacked Meredith's faith in God and His dealings and leading, said it was strange and they wished that they could have Meredith's faith. Skeptics remarked that it was mere coincidence. But Meredith *knew* and all the rest of her life she thanked God because He had led her there.

It was a cloudless spring day and the joy of spring was in her heart as she rattled along in her ancient car. She hummed a little chorus which she had learned at a youth meeting.

> He's able, He's able,
> I know He's able.
> I know my Lord is able
> To carry me through.

The road wound through a wooded section shaded by giant oaks which cast a shifting pattern of light and shadow as the sun shone through their gnarled branches. In the distance she saw the grim outlines of the state prison. The iron-barred windows reflected the light of the sun but Meredith knew that those within the dingy walls had no light within their souls. Her heart reached out in pity for the hundreds within those walls. There were hardened criminals in the prison, of course, men who killed ruthlessly, men who had committed every crime, but still, she mused, Christ had died for them and their souls were precious in His sight.

If they could only know what the peace of God could mean to their sin-laden, tortured hearts! If they could only realize what it would mean to have all the bitterness and evil and lust wiped from their hearts and minds when the light from Calvary shone within.

Her thoughts were interrupted by a sizzling sound and a sudden wobbling of the front wheels. A front tire had gone flat and here she was in the middle of nowhere, off the main highway and with no one in sight. She got out and stared at the flat tire. The shabby little car looked crestfallen and dejected as it drooped to one side.

"Of all the stupid things for you to do," she addressed the tire. "Why couldn't you have lasted just a few more miles? Now what am I going to do?"

She had feared that this would happen, for the tires were old, but she hoped for the best when she set out on the trip and since she had come this far without trouble, she felt that they would hold out the rest of the way.

She opened the trunk and stared disconsolately at the spare. She knew that even if she could get it out of the car, she wouldn't be able to put it on. Tears came to her eyes but she brushed them away as she valiantly repeated a verse that was one of her favorites: "All things work together for good to those who love the Lord. . . ."

"I don't know how they can, Lord," she murmured as she looked at the tire, "but I do believe."

How could they, she wondered, as she looked about her hopelessly. She was at least five miles from town and cars seldom passed this way. She would either have to sit here perhaps for hours, waiting for help or else walk to town and leave her beloved car to the mercy of some possible thief. She had taken this road because it was a short cut to town, but she regretted it now.

While she stood there wondering what to do, she heard a faint sound in the distance like the chug of a motor. She turned and looked hopefully down the road, She uttered a sigh of relief as she saw a truck approaching. As it drew nearer she stepped out into the road and waved her hands.

The truck came to a stop with a screeching of brakes and the driver sat there staring at her silently.

She was well worth looking at, for she possessed a piquancy and a sparkling, glowing personality which was far more attractive than mere beauty. Her hair shone in the warm sun with a golden-brown sheen and her eyes which were dark brown and fringed with long curling lashes were large and lustrous. Her mouth was small and seemed made for laughter. When she smiled, her whole face radiated with the beauty of that smile and she was smiling at the occupant of the truck now. She did not realize how her presence and her charm affected him. She was not thinking of how she looked, nor of the rapt look of admiration which he cast upon her. She was thinking of that flat tire and of how worried her aunt would be if she did not arrive when she was expected.

"I wonder if you would mind helping me," she said as the driver continued to stare silently at her as if he were hypnotized. "My front tire has gone flat and I don't have the strength to get that wheel off."

The driver gave a sudden start as if he had suddenly wakened from some hypnotic spell and jumped down from the truck.

"Of course I'll help you," he said. "Do you have a jack?"

"Oh! I don't think I have," she confessed. "I believe I left mine out when I was cleaning the car trunk. I do hope you have one."

"Yes, I have one," and he turned to get it.

She noticed that he was good-looking, in spite of the rather soiled dungarees and the close cropped hair which was so unbecoming.

He got out the jack and went to work silently. Soon he had the wheel off. Now that the tension was relieved and help had come, she relaxed and watched him with interest. He really was handsome, she said to herself. If he had on decent clothes and didn't have that awful crew cut, he would be something to look at! She wondered who he was and if he lived in Cedarville. She hoped she could find out before they parted.

"I was just wondering if I would have to walk all the way into town," she said as he worked. She was hoping to lead up to something that would enlighten her. "This road isn't used often. I knew that, but I knew it would cut off several miles and I was anxious to get to my aunt's as soon as possible. I'm already late and she will be worried about me."

He made no reply and she felt frustrated but she would not give up.

"You have no idea how glad I am that you came along," she said.

"I'm glad I can be of service," he replied without looking at her.

His voice was cold and almost forbidding. Its undertone of bitterness made her wonder. What was wrong? Was she bothering him or was he angry because he had had to stop and help her?

"I'm sorry to be of so much trouble," she said contritely. "I hope I'm not delaying you so that you'll not be on time wherever you're going."

He shrugged. "What does it matter?" The bitterness was more evident. "I have nothing else but time."

She was hoping that he would say more, but there was only silence.

"I'm going to live with my aunt," she began once more, hopefully. "My aunt and uncle are Mr. and Mrs. Barton. I wonder if, by any chance, you know them."

He shook his head without replying. He tightened up the bolts on the wheel and removed the jack, then tested the bolts again and put the other wheel in the trunk, then closed the lid.

"How I do thank you!" she said fervently as he turned to get into the truck. "Won't you — will — you please let me pay you for your trouble?" she stammered.

She was afraid it might offend him, but she could not let him go without offering to pay him. She wished he wouldn't go without even looking at her or saying another word. That grim look in his eyes in the brief moments he had met hers after that first hypnotic stare, together with the set of his lips and his whole bearing, aroused her interest and her sympathy. She felt that he must be desperately unhappy and it stirred a desire within her to help him, to take away that unhappiness. She wished that she could share with him the peace and joy which had been hers since she was a child and had accepted Christ as her Saviour.

It had always been that way with her, the desire to tell others how they might have what she possessed. Sometimes it had gotten her into trouble, for often she was made to realize that the ones she spoke to did not want to be told and they answered her in no uncertain tones.

When he turned from her without a word, she was eager to know his name. He had wakened an interest in her which was not entirely spiritual, but quite human. She had never met anyone quite like him. She overlooked the soiled dungarees and his hands which were now dirty. She saw only the youth and strength in the well-built figure, the handsome face even though its expression was so bitter, the gray eyes with that forbidding light in them, and the whole intrigued her.

His face flushed for a moment at her words and he met her eyes again. Again that brief look of admiration shone through them, but at once the stern light returned as he answered.

"I couldn't take money for helping a person in trouble," he said.

"But I've been such a bother," she argued, "and I'm sorry to have caused you trouble. I appreciate it so much. How can I ever repay you?"

"Just forget me," he said harshly, then as he saw the hurt look in her eyes he added, "it was nothing really."

"But it was to me," she persisted. "You have no idea what a big help it was. My name is Meredith Baxter," and she held out her hand. "Would you mind telling me who has been kind enough to help me in trouble?"

Her smile was winsome and appealing and her eyes looked into his with a warm, friendly glow that brought a flush to his face. He wiped his hand on his trouser leg and took hers for a brief moment.

"My name is Bill," he said.

Bill. What a help that was!

She watched him as he got into the truck and drove away

without looking at her. She felt chilled and rebuffed. He really had been rude. What was wrong with him? Her heart sank as she thought that perhaps she would never see him again. Why had he appealed to her so strongly when he had been so uncivil? No one had ever treated her like that before. In fact, all of the boys she had ever met had fallen over themselves to be agreeable.

"Meredith Baxter, you're a silly little dunce to bother about that fellow," she chided herself as she started the car and once more rattled toward town. "He's probably just an ignorant fellow who hates the world and everyone in it because he isn't a millionaire or something."

She knew this wasn't true. That young man was no ignorant lout. But there was something in his heart which shouldn't be there. She wondered if she would ever know what it was — if she would ever see him again.

As the truck rolled down the road, its driver was talking aloud to himself.

"Bill Gordon, you should be ashamed of yourself! That girl was trying to be friendly and you wouldn't even be civil to her. She'll probably despise you. Why did you do it? She was so beautiful and she looked so hurt when you were such a rude, uncivil brute."

He knew deep within his own bitter heart why he did it. She would really despise him if she knew the truth. How he had longed to detain her and hear the sound of her soft musical voice and revel in her beauty! She was the first girl he had talked to in so long that it seemed like a breath from heaven to hear her voice. Heaven! Bah! Why use that word? There was no such place and life here for him was the only hell he believed in.

He turned in at the prison gate and nodded to the guard who locked the gate after him. When he stopped the truck another guard came up as he prepared to unload.

"You're late, Bill," the fellow said. "What happened?"

"Stopped to help someone who had a flat tire," Bill answered.

The fellow turned away. Bill set his lips and the cold

light returned to his eyes. He resolultey determined to forget that soft voice and those luminous brown eyes and that smile which illumined a girlish face and made it even more beauti-ful. Such things were not for him. But how could he control a rebellious memory which persisted in recalling a vision that had come like a sudden light in a darkened sky?

CHAPTER 2

CEDARVILLE WAS LIKE MANY OTHER TOWNS of medium size in the South, too small to be called a city, yet too large to be classed as a village. The business section was centered around the traditional courthouse square where the loafers congregated under the shade of the ancient oaks to see what was going on and to gossip idly about trivialities. Excitement rarely disturbed the tranquility of the orderly happenings. Occasionally the prison car drove through with a new group of inmates for the penitentiary nearby, but that was nothing to cause even a ripple among those who had seen that car go back and forth through the years.

On visiting days at the prison, people came in their own cars or on the bus. Some of them remained at the hotel overnight but most of them were not able to pay for hotel accommodations and they either returned the same day or slept in one of the cheap rooming houses on the edge of town. The prison truck made its daily trip for supplies. Occasionally the driver would answer the greetings that were waved to him from some of the loafers, but more often he would ignore them as he kept his eyes fixed upon the road ahead.

The streets in the residential section were wide and tree-lined and the houses were well-kept and attractive and their gardens were flower-laden all through spring and summer.

Meredith stopped her car in front of one of the better homes. The front door opened and her aunt, Mrs. Barton, hurried out to meet her.

"My, my, child! How worried I've been!" she exclaimed as she took Meredith in her arms and kissed her. "I've been looking for you for hours. I was afraid something terrible had happened."

"Something did happen," Meredith told her. "I had a flat tire and I would probably have had to walk here if someone hadn't come along and helped me. I took the old road because it was shorter, but I was sorry until that truck driver came along and changed the wheel for me."

"It was lucky for you that he did, for scarcely anyone ever uses that road, now that the highway is finished. Except visitors to the prison."

"It wasn't luck, Aunt Mary," Meredith said seriously. "I'm sure it was God."

"Have it your way," Mrs. Barton conceded. "I still believe in luck, even if you do maintain that everything is in God's hands and that there is no such thing as luck. I know you're tired, but I want to hear everything that has happened since I left you. I'll have Sam get your things and put them in your room."

Meredith followed her aunt into the large comfortable living room and sat down in one of the inviting arm chairs while her aunt gave an order to a maid who had appeared when they came in. Meredith admitted that she was tired for she had driven far and she had been under a strain for fear that the tires would not hold out. Presently the maid came in with glasses of iced root beer and she sipped the drink while her aunt plied her with questions.

"So you decided to rent the house instead of selling it," Mrs. Barton commented. "I thought it would be better for you to get it off your hands, for rented property can sometimes be a great worry."

"I had thought I would sell it," Meredith said, "and I had a buyer for it, but when it came down to the decision, I just couldn't part with the dear old home. It held too many precious memories. I couldn't turn it over to a stranger to own. Someday I may be able to go back there and live. When the ache of Granny's death is not quite so keen."

"I was hoping that you would be satisfied to stay here with us," her aunt said with disappointment in her voice.

"Oh, I shall be, Aunt Mary," Meredith hastened to say. "Perhaps I'll never go back there. But for now, I just couldn't sell it. An elderly couple who knew Granny and loved her are going to rent it and I know they'll take care of the place because they loved her." Her smile flashed from her lips and her eyes as she added, "Perhaps someday when I am married, I'll go back there and raise my children in the old home where I grew up."

Mrs. Barton's face brightened. "You'll have many a chance of getting married here, for there are lots of eligible young men. I have a nice young man already picked out for you and I'm sure that when he sees how lovely you are he'll fall head over heels in love with you."

Meredith's musical laughter rippled out. "And who is this young man who will fall an easy victim to my charms?"

"He's young Terry Stuart. His uncle is the warden at the prison. He's the warden's deputy just now, but he's studying law and he will make a name for himself someday soon, I'm sure. He comes from an old aristocratic family. He's good looking and he's also a good church member. That ought to add much to his favor," and Mrs. Barton smiled. "I'll have him over to meet you soon."

"Sounds good, all but the prison connection," Meredith remarked. "I'll look him over, but just now I'm not in the mood for romance. Hadn't I better get my things unpacked? I'm sure all my clothes are terribly wrinkled."

"You can get them out and Susan can press them for you," her aunt replied as they rose and ascended the stairs to the room Meredith was to occupy.

The room was large and airy, with the high ceiling typical of old homes of the South. A thick carpet covered the floor and the four-poster bed was attractive with a ruffled organdy spread.

"What a lovely room!" Meredith remarked. "It is so good of you to want me to come and stay with you until I can sort of get my bearings," and she gave her aunt a loving hug.

"I want you to stay here, not for just a while, but until you do get married," her aunt said. "Please don't talk as if you were here just on a visit. You know that your uncle and I are lonely and it will be wonderful to have a young person here in the house with us."

"We won't argue about it now," Meredith said as she kissed her aunt lightly upon her cheek. "I must get these clothes out and see what has to be done to them."

She unpacked her bags and laid her dresses on the bed and looked them over. They were hopelessly wrinkled and Meredith uttered a sigh.

"I'm the world's worst packer," she said as she eyed the clothes.

"Susan will put them back into shape for you," said her aunt as she rang a bell near the door. In answer the maid appeared and stood waiting for instructions.

"Susan, this is Miss Meredith," Mrs. Barton said.

Susan bowed and Meredith said, "I'm glad to know you, Susan. You surely have made this room spotless and lovely for me."

The maid smiled and murmured a "thank you."

"Take Meredith's dresses and press them for her," Mrs. Barton said.

Meredith protested. "Aunt Mary, please let me do them. I can really do a good job of pressing, even if I can't pack. And I must have something to do. I can't just sit around and let you and Susan wait on me."

"You'll have plenty to do when you get acquainted with the young people," Mrs. Barton assured her. "They always have something on hand to keep them from getting bored. Besides, you need a rest after that long vigil you had with your grandmother. Sit down and tell me about it all," and she indicated a chair.

Meredith obeyed while Susan took the dresses out.

"You surely have had a trying time of it all these long months," Mrs. Barton observed. "I'm sure you feel relieved, now that it is all over, for it was such a trial when she was helpless and required such constant care."

"Why, no, Aunt Mary," Meredith protested. "It was no trial. It was a privilege for me to be able to help her when she needed me, after all she has done for me. I loved doing it and if I could have kept her with me, I would have been glad to do all I could to ease her suffering. I miss her so terribly that sometimes I feel I can't stand it.'' Tears came to her eyes and a sob choked her.

"I know, child," Mrs. Barton said tenderly as she reached out and patted Meredith's hand. "It was stupid of me to say that. I know how much you loved her."

"She was all I've had all these years. You know that I can scarcely remember Mother. She was not only mother and father to me but she led me to the Lord and it was she who taught me to believe that one day we shall meet again, perhaps sooner than we think."

Mrs. Barton was silent. She did not respond to Meredith's words for, though she was a church member and attended services regularly, she did not share her niece's faith and Meredith's words left her heart cold and unresponsive.

"You are fortunate that your grandmother left you well-provided for, so that you will never have to worry about money," she remarked.

Meredith's eyes glowed through the mist of tears and a smile crept across her trembling lips.

"Yes, she left me well-provided for, not only with money, but with something far more precious than anything that money could buy. She left me her Bible that she taught me to love. She taught me how to receive the gift of eternal life because she taught me to believe the truths in that Book."

Mrs. Barton hastened to change the subject. She could not remember where her Bible was. She couldn't remember when she had last opened its pages and read from it.

"Suppose we go downstairs and wait for your uncle," she said. "He'll becoming home before long. It's cool and shady on the porch. Unless you'd rather lie down for a while," she added.

"No, I'm not tired enough for that," Meredith replied and they went down to the front porch and sat chatting until Mr. Barton came home.

Mrs. Barton was the sister of Meredith's father. He died when Meredith was a baby and in just a few years after that Meredith's mother had died, leaving Meredith to the care of her grandmother. Meredith had loved "Granny" as her own mother and the grandmother had not only lavished love upon her, but had, as Meredith said, given her something infinitely more precious. She had instilled into her heart and mind the promises in God's Word and the desire which led her to accept Christ as her Saviour.

After the old lady's death, Mrs. Barton had insisted that Meredith should come and live with them and Meredith was glad to get away for a while at least, from the loneliness of the old house which held so many precious memories that now were too painful for her to endure.

On Saturday evening the town was alive with people who came from nearby farms and smaller communities and the streets were crowded. Stores remained open until a late hour and were thronged with those who bought and those who just came in to look around.

Meredith decided to go to town and join the throngs. It would be a diversion and she felt the need of exercise after sitting and relaxing for two days. It was not quite dark when she reached the business section and she strolled along, looking into shop windows and watching the people passing by.

Suddenly her gaze was arrested by the sight of a truck which came to a stop in front of one of the hardware stores. The driver got out and went inside. It was Bill. She waited hopefully for him to come out. Perhaps he would see her and she might be able to have a word with him. Her hope was not realized. He came out presently carrying a heavy package. He put it in the truck and then got in and started off without even glancing in her direction. She opened her mouth impulsively to call to him, but she realized how foolish that would be. He would certainly misunderstand.

As she watched him ride away a sense of frustration swept over her. She could not forget the look in those gray eyes and the set of his lips and in spite of his rudeness, she could not help but be interested in him. Something deep and bitter held him in its grip. How she wished that she could find out what it was and perhaps help him to believe that there was a balm for every sorrow and a healing for every bitter wound!

CHAPTER 3

ON SUNDAY MORNING, after a late breakfast, Mr. and
Mrs. Barton prepared for church. There were several
churches in the town, each of them old and with well-
established pastors and members. Cars of every type and
vintage made their way down the tree-shaded streets to the
various places of worship. Cedarville was a church-going
community. The citizens felt that it was not only a duty for
them as church members, but it gave one a certain feeling of
dignity and respect to be seen going to the house of worship
on Sunday morning. At night, of course, it was a different
story. The majority thought that they had made the necessary concession to the God they were supposed to worship
when they attended the morning service. In the evening there
were television and radio and social gatherings among the
older members and much less quiet gatherings among the
younger set.

Several of the churches had given up the attempt to hold
evening services, for the pastors were weary of preaching to
empty pews with just a handful of those who were faithful
enough to be there.

What a contrast this was, Meredith thought, as she
drove with her aunt and uncle to their place of worship, to the
church she had attended all her life. There had been a succession of preachers there during the twenty years of her life, but
each one had been chosen after a careful searching and a
prayerful questioning on the part of the board members. And

each one had been fired with a zeal that not only enabled him to give out a message that encouraged the believers, but which won the lost to Christ.

Meredith had wanted to go to Sunday school, for she had always attended, but her aunt told her that the Sunday school was so small and so uninteresting that she was sure Meredith would not enjoy it.

The prospect was not encouraging to Meredith and when she sat during the long and tedious service, the future, as far as her church life was concerned, seemed dismal indeed. The congregation appeared properly attentive to the sermon but Meredith wondered how they could be. She found it hard to keep her mind on what the preacher was saying. He had read a short text and then wandered far afield as he expanded upon various happenings in the world and drew conclusions which surely did not agree with what she had been taught and which she knew to be true from her own reading of the Bible.

How could this man be so blind to the truth, she wondered, as he continued to give his views concerning a better world when all sin would be overcome by education and stricter laws, by presenting a better way of life among the brotherhood of men in the nations which were now bitterly opposed to everything American? How could people sit and appear interested when she wanted to cry out, ''That is not what the Bible says! It says that the world will grow worse instead of better and that wars will not cease until the Prince of peace comes to take possession of His throne and rule the world.''

No wonder people did not want to come back again to a night service when the message gave them no inspiration, no desire to live better lives and to love their Lord and serve Him more faithfully because of Calvary. This preacher did not once mention the name of Jesus. What a difference from the sermons she had heard all her life! She could sit and listen to those other sermons while her soul responded to the exposition of the Word so ably presented, while her heart overflowed with love and the desire to better serve the One who had suffered and died for her.

She turned and looked at her aunt and uncle. Mrs. Barton's eyes were fixed glassily upon the preacher who intoned his words monotonously and unconvincingly. She saw that her uncle was nodding. Others in the congregation were folllowing suit. She couldn't blame them. She felt that she too would go to sleep if she were not so indignant that a man should so waste God's time and the time of his people by such inane nonsense. He did nothing but kill time. She wondered what would happen to this man when he stood before the Lord to give an account of his stewardship. She doubted if he would ever stand before Christ as a saved person. Surely if he had anything to give he would give it out. How many other preachers were there, she wondered, who were doing just this same thing today? There were lost souls in this large congregation, yet he was doing nothing to win them to the Lord. How could he, if he himself was not saved? He couldn't be, or he wouldn't be giving out this trivial untruth, this poor excuse for a gospel message.

Her eyes wandered over the congregation again and she found herself looking into the eyes of a young man who was looking intently at her. There was unconcealed admiration in his gaze and he did not turn his eyes away when their glances met. Meredith lowered her eyes and she felt the color stealing into her cheeks. She wanted to peep at him again, for he was quite good-looking, but she dared not. She returned her gaze to the preacher, trying to appear interested.

At last the sermon was ended and they stood for the closing hymn. She uttered a sigh of relief. How was she going to endure this sort of thing for as long as she remained with her aunt? In her heart there surged a longing for the old home even though it was now empty, and for the inspiring sermons and for the friends who were wonderful and who loved her Lord as she did. But she remembered that vacant place where her beloved Granny had sat for many years and swift pain filled her heart. She couldn't go back there now. Not just yet, at least. But as soon as she felt that she could stand to face these memories, she would go back. She would wither and die, spiritually, in this atmosphere.

As they filed out of the church, pausing while her aunt

and uncle greeted friends, the owner of those admiring eyes approached and greeted Mrs. Barton with an engaging smile.

"I'm waiting for that promised introduction," he said as he shook hands with her.

"Why, of course, Terry," Mrs. Barton answered with a pleased smile. "Mr. Stuart, allow me to introduce you to my niece, Meredith Baxter."

Meredith acknowledged the introduction as Terry Stuart smiled at her.

"Isn't she all that I told you she would be?" Mrs. Barton gurgled happily. She had seen the look in Terry's eyes.

"All and much more," he replied with his admiring eyes upon Meredith.

"Really, Aunt Mary," Meredith protested, "you make me feel like a museum piece on exhibition. What else is there for him to say?"

"Much more, if I dared," Terry said with an ardent look.

Meredith was not flattered by the compliment. In fact, she resented it. How stupid must he think she was, to be pleased? She turned without replying or giving him an answering smile.

"How about having dinner with us?" Mrs. Barton asked. "We would love to have you, wouldn't we, Meredith?"

"That is entirely up to you, Aunt Mary," Meredith returned indifferently.

Terry Stuart did not appear to notice her indifference, but accepted the invitation with alacrity.

"Thank you for asking me," he said. "I shall be glad to come. I am fortunate to have the afternoon off."

Meredith did not look forward with much joy to the afternoon ahead of her. Though this young man was quite good-looking, he did not appeal to her in the least. She had looked forward to reading and answering some letters. Now she would be forced to make conversation with someone for whom it did not seem worth while.

She was relieved to find that she did not have to exert

herself to make conversation. Terry, somewhat to her surprise, proved an entertaining talker and was well-informed upon many interesting topics. Before she realized it, she was enjoying herself and told him truthfully when he rose to leave, that she had enjoyed his visit.

"May I come to see you again real soon?" he asked.

"Why, of course," Mrs. Barton interposed. "I'm sure Meredith will be glad to have you call whenever you can. I want her to meet the young people and to enjoy herself. I shall turn her over to you and I shall expect you to see that she has a good time."

"I shall be glad to do my best to make her enjoy herself," he said, then added with a smile, "but I am not sure that I want her to meet too many other boys. I'm afraid that I shall be a little selfish along that line."

Meredith did not smile. He could have left that unsaid! What did he think she was, a stupid little nincompoop, just waiting for compliments to be thrown at her?

He saw that she was not impressed at his clumsy attempt to flatter her and his face flushed.

"What do you say, Miss Baxter? That I may call again?" he asked.

She gave him a rather chill smile as she said, "What can I say but yes?" Then she realized that she was being rude and hastened to add, "Of course I shall be glad to have you call again."

When he had left, her aunt turned to her, smiling broadly.

"You've made quite an impression upon Terry," she said. "But I knew you would. What do you think of him? Don't you like him?"

Meredith shrugged. "He's good-looking, just as you said, but I'm not a bit enthused about him."

"Why, Meredith! I thought you would be sure to like him. He's quite a catch and almost any girl would be thrilled to have him look at her the way he looked at you."

"I may be sorry to deprive them of that thrill," Meredith replied.

Mrs. Barton looked at her speculatively. "Do you have

a boy friend back home?''

Meredith smiled. "Lots of them. And good-looking ones, too. But they're only friends and I'm not in love with any of them, if that's what is worrying you."

"That is some satisfaction," Mrs. Barton admitted. "I'm going to do my best to see that you get a husband who will keep you here. I don't want to lose you, my dear, now that I've had you even this little while." She put an arm around Meredith and hugged her.

With annoying persistence Meredith's thoughts returned to Bill. She was provoked that she should be curious and interested in someone who had been rude and who, in all probability she would never know any better than she did now. In the light of what happened in the anxiety and tension of the months ahead of her and when she looked back upon the events which changed so many lives, she knew that there was a purpose and a plan in it all. And she knew that it was God.

In the days which followed this first Sunday, when she had time to be alone, her thoughts wandered to this unknown young man and she wondered how she could find out more about him. There was not much time for her thoughts to wander, for her aunt did not give her many hours alone. With the mistaken idea that Meredith must be kept entertained so that she would forget her sorrow and learn to be happy and content in her new home, she was either planning something for Meredith to do or else insisting upon entertaining her with her own ceaseless chatter.

Meredith protested that she didn't have to be constantly on the go, that she could be satisfied to be alone with a good book or just sitting quietly on the porch watching the passersby. She soon gave up the idea of trying to help with the housework, for neither Mrs. Barton nor Susan would allow her to do anything.

True to his promise to see that Meredith was not lonely, Terry came to see her a few evenings later. He brought flowers which Meredith received graciously. As they sat on the front porch and talked, she listened to his interesting conversation and she thought that perhaps she had ben wrong to misjudge him as she had done at first. Her first antagonism gradually faded and she thought that perhaps she would enjoy his friendship. She knew, even in this short time that she would never be satisfied to live in Cedarville always and Terry would be an entertaining friend while she remained there.

After a while Terry asked her if she would go for a ride with him. She noticed that they took the old road as they left town, instead of the New highway.

"I like this road because it is less traveled than the other," he remarked. "I can pay more attention to you and not have to watch the traffic so closely."

She did not answer and he mistook her silence. One hand left the wheel and his arm stole around her. She straightened and turned upon him indignantly as she drew away from him.

"If that is the reason you took this road, please turn back, unless you want me to get out and walk home," she said.

He withdrew his arm quickly and said apologetically, "I'm sorry. I thought you understood. I thought you rather expected it."

"Why should you think that!" she exclaimed indignantly. "I've certainly given you no indication that I expected it. I've only known you a few days and this is only the second time we've been together."

He laughed rather sheepishly and explained lamely.

"I'm sorry. I was mistaken. Other girls I've been with expected it. After all, time means nothing and you are lovely. I thought you were like the rest."

"Well, I'm not," she retorted. "and if those others are like you say they are, I'm glad I'm not like them."

"You really are different," he remarked. "But what a cold heart you must have! Don't you ever want love and affection, or is your heart just a lump of ice?"

"Do you call this love?" she blazed. "Yes, I want love and I want affection and someday I hope to have both from some man I may fall in love with and who not only loves me and wants to give me affection, but who also respects me.

This isn't love and it isn't affection. It's degrading to any girl who has any self respect and no girl who permits it has the respect that she should receive.''

"You're a strange person," he said. "I've never met anyone quite like you. I apologize for misjudging you. Your ideas are just a little bit old-fashioned and out-of-date in this modern world."

"But they are mine, nevertheless, and I don't intend to change them. If I'm so strange and out of date and such a disappointment to you, perhaps we'd better turn back. I think both of us would be glad if you did."

"On the contrary, I would be disappointed if you refused to go on with me," he stated firmly. "I promise you that I shall not offend you again. And I assure you that you have my deepest respect. I want to know you better."

She turned to him with a smile.

"Then let's be friends. I do want friends, for I miss the ones I left in my old home and I think sometimes that I never should have left there, even though it was so terrible to be there without Granny."

"I want to be your friend," he said seriously. "Perhaps someday I may hope to be more than a friend."

She turned to him with quick words of rebuke upon her lips but she did not utter them, for she saw something in his eyes that silenced her.

"That is no inane compliment," he said as his serious eyes met hers. "I realized that first day that you did not enjoy them. I'm serious, Meredith. May I call you that?"

"Of course," she assented.

"I shall not force my attentions upon you, but I mean it when I say that I hope to be more than your friend. Friendship is all I ask for now."

"That is all you need expect," she said decisively.

He was silent for a time as they drove slowly along the almost deserted road. Presently she saw the lights of the prison and the grim outlines of its wall showing shadowy and forbidding in the approaching darkness.

"I believe that is where you work," Meredith remarked as they drew nearer.

"Yes, but only temporarily," he hastened to reply. "My uncle is the warden, as you perhaps know. His deputy is on a long leave due to illness, so I'm acting in his place. I hope to finish my law course by the end of next year and then I'll be on my own. I'll be glad to be out of that foul place. It's degrading to be in such close contact with those beasts of crime."

"When you become a full-fledged lawyer, perhaps you won't think of those prisoners as beasts. Some of them may become your clients," she said.

"Not those fellows," he asserted. "My line will be different. I wouldn't raise my little finger to help one of them escape what they deserve. Some of them in there now should be sitting in the electric chair."

"Some of them have never had a chance to be anything. If someone had only told them about the Lord, perhaps they wouldn't be there now," she remarked sadly.

He laughed derisively. "What an idea! They wouldn't be any different, no matter what chances they might have had. They're just rotten all the way through, just bad through and through."

"So are all of us, without Christ," she said. "Have you never thought of that?" Her serious gaze bored deep into his.

"No, I'm afraid I never have," he admitted, taken aback by her words. "I don't think I know just what you mean."

And yet he was such a good church member, she thought.

She did not try to enlighten him and he hastened to change the subject. She was glad that he did. This was neither the time nor the place for her to try to explain.

CHAPTER 4

TERRY DID HIS BEST TO MAKE AMENDS for his blunder. He hoped that he could wipe out the impression which he knew he had left upon Meredith. Even though she had said she wanted him for a friend, he was keen enough to read the cold appraisal of him in her eyes and her distrust even in her handshake when they parted.

He came as often as she would allow him and always brought flowers or candy and when he dared ask her to go for a ride with him again, he kept their conversation as impersonal as possible. He was eager to see the warm light of friendship in her lovely eyes. Her rebuff and sharp rebuke had done just the opposite from what it would ordinarily have done if any other girl he had ever known had done what she had done; it aroused a respect for her which he had had for no other girl.

Every one of these girls, many of them as pretty as Meredith, had been so eager to please him and to keep him at her side as an admirer, that she had yielded to his caresses and his lips unashamed, and though this had satisfied his vanity over his conquests, deep within him there was a contempt for these silly girls who would so shamelessly yield themselves to a man's embrace and his careless kiss, in hope of winning his love.

It was true, as Meredith had said, that this was not love. It was in reality degrading both to him and to the girl who threw herself at him. Why had he not seen this before? Possibly because he did not want to, for he was intent only upon satisfying his vanity by his powers of conquest. He

29

knew that he was attractive to the opposite sex and it gave him a sense of power to know that no girl could resist him. He had never considered any of them seriously until he met Meredith.

When he saw how displeased she was at his clumsy compliments, it rather surprised him. Any other girl he had known, instead of freezing him with her cold glance, would have smiled and invited more silly compliments. Meredith's indifference to his charm had intrigued him but when she rebuked him so severely for daring to think that she wanted his caresses, he was distinctly interested. As the days passed and he began to know her better, this interest grew into something stronger.

He had told her that he hoped one day to be something more than a friend, but this was only in line with what had grown to be a habit. He had said that to so many girls before her that he said it to her through force of habit. Her answer had made him realize that her attitude was no mere act, but the real manifestation of her nature and her ideas which he had not taken seriously at first. He began to realize that what he had said through force of habit had become true. He wanted desperately to be more than her friend. He knew that he was falling in love with her.

After a while Meredith ceased to be on her guard when she was with him. She felt that he really wanted to be friends and she was willing to accept him on these terms, for she was lonely. The girls she had met had not been too cordial. The fact that Terry had turned his attention to Meredith did not add to her popularity with them. Even though Terry was only a deputy at the prison, he belonged to one of the oldest and most prominent families in the town and his future as a lawyer would be assured, for one of his uncles was a judge in the district court.

Mrs. Barton was immensely pleased that Terry seemed interested in Meredith and she did all in her power to prosper his cause with Meredith. She invited him to dinner whenever he was present at the morning church service and he accepted eagerly. Meredith knew what her aunt was hoping and she did not have the heart to discourage her, but she knew that

Terry could never be anything more than a friend. She found him entertaining and she appreciated his flowers and candy and his attentions, but she did nothing to encourage him to hope for more than friendship. Sometimes she felt guilty when she caught a certain look in his eyes which told her more than his lips dared utter, but, she argued, since she had told him not to hope for more, there was no harm in continuing their relationship.

Other boys admired her from a distance, but when they saw how attentive Terry was, they did not try to date her. According to their code, she belonged to him, for the present at least. Meredith recognized this and wished she could do something to change the situation but she could do nothing. She decided, however, to speak to her aunt about it.

"I wish there were something I could do to make the boys and girls like me," she said. "The girls all give me the cold shoulder and the boys all treat me as if I had the plague or something."

"Why, I thought you were satisfied with Terry," Mrs. Barton remarked in surprise.

"Well, I'm not. I want the companionship of some girl friends and I don't want to be tied down to one boy as if I were emgaged to him."

"I'm sure it would please Terry if that should be true," Mrs. Barton remarked. "I believe he's in love with you. That is the reason all the other boys have kept away."

"Then I shall stop seeing Terry," Meredith stated. "I don't love him and I never can love him. He's not my type and besides he's not a Christian."

"Not a Christian!" her aunt echoed in shocked tones. "How can you say that? There's not a more faithful member of the church than that young man. Next year, I'm sure he will be elected to the board."

"That doesn't mean that he's a Christian," Meredith told her. "He doesn't even know what it means to be born again."

"He may not agree with your ideas of religion, but does that mean that he's not a Christian? I'm afraid you're rather narrow-minded, my child. That, of course, is natural, being so much in your grandmother's company. She had old-fashioned ideas about religion, but times have changed and we have a more modern approach to God these days. I'm sure that Terry is as much a Christian as any member of the church.''

Meredith could not repress a smile. ''He could be that and still not be a Christian,'' she remarked. ''From what I've heard of the sermons he's had handed out to him, it's not surprising that he doesn't know the first requisite of being a Christian.''

''And what is the first requisite, pray tell me,'' Mrs. Barton said with eyes suddenly gone cold and a voice that was disapproving in the extreme.

''What it has always been, Aunt Mary. Times may have changed but God's Word has not changed and there is no modern approach to God. We have to come to Him in the same way that Granny did years ago, the same way that she taught me to approach Him, the same way everyone has to come if they ever expect to have salvation and the hope of heaven.''

Mrs. Barton regarded her niece with appraising eyes and she spoke still more coldly.

''Do you mean to say that I have no right to a hope of going to heaven?''

''I have no right to judge you, Auntie, but I do know that there is only one way to receive that hope or to claim it and that is by receiving the gift of salvation and eternal life through Jesus Christ. And the only way to receive that is by confessing to Him that one is a sinner and asking for forgiveness, believing His word and receiving Him into your heart. Unless you have done that, you cannot hope to go to heaven and if you have that hope without Christ in your heart, that hope is vain.''

''Nonsense!'' Mrs. Barton exploded. ''Rev. Hawthorne says that a man's destiny lies within his own being and that if he is faithful to the best that is within him, he need have no fear of the future. God will reward him for his faithfulness. He is a brainy man and I'd rather believe what he says than any old worn-out ideas that your grandmother has taught you.''

''It is not that Granny taught it to me, but it's what the Bible says,'' Meredith insisted.

There was a touch of sadness in her voice. How could she ever convince this self-satisfied, spiritually-blinded aunt whom she loved, that she was a lost soul, on her way to eternal punishment? What a terrible judgment awaited the brainy Rev. Hawthorne if he did not repent and lead his congregation in the right way, instead of filling their minds and hearts with false doctrine and untruths!

A silence fell between them and Meredith could feel her aunt's displeasure.

''I'm sorry if I have said anything to hurt you, Auntie dear,'' she said going over to her aunt and kissing her cheek. ''I was only saying what I know to be true and what is so dear to my heart. I don't know what I would do if I didn't have the peace of God within me, for my heart is torn with grief over Granny's going.''

''That's all right, child,'' Mrs. Barton replied, giving Meredith a hug. ''Let's say no more about it. You have your belief and I have mine. We're all striving to get to the same place and I'm sure that in the end we'll all be there if we do what we think is best.''

The same old sophistry, Meredith thought, the same thing that she had heard so many times before from others to whom she had talked about God. But she did not reply to this. Wisdom told her not to. Arguments would not help. Only the Holy Spirit could prepare the way in her aunt's heart for the truth and until that time came, she would not force her views upon her aunt.

''We got way off the subject,'' Meredith said. ''I want to have the friendship of some other boys and girls. How can I get them to be more friendly?''

''I'll see what we can do,'' Mrs. Barton replied. I'll invite some of the young people here for a little party. This house is not suitable for dancing, but we could have a few tables of bridge. Or I could have a dinner dance for you at the country club. I had thought of that before, but I thought that perhaps you wouldn't want any parties so soon after your grandmother's death."

"I don't believe in those long periods of mourning," Meredith said. "I grieve for Granny, but since I know that she is with the Lord and is so happy there with Him, there is no reason why I should seclude myself in hopeless mourning. I want to forget my loneliness and the ache of being without her. Being with friends helps one to forget. But I couldn't let you have a card party or a dance for me, because I don't play cards and I don't dance."

"Well! Then what do you do?" Mrs. Barton exclaimed with eyes wide with amazement. "All the young people that I know do those things."

Meredith smiled. "I found many things to do at home. I taught Sunday school and often I took the children to the park for picnics. I played tennis and basketball and I went swimming with my Girl Scouts, I went to musicals and I had my radio and my books. In between times I visited the hospital and witnessed to those who would let me talk to them. Once a month I went to the prison with a group and we sang choruses and gave testimonies and had the joy of seeing some of the prisoners accept the Lord."

"M'm!" was Mrs. Barton's only comment.

"How would it do to have a picnic at the lake and then go for a speed boat ride afterwards?" Meredith ventured to suggest.

"If that is what you want," her aunt said. "I'll invite just a small group so that you can get better acquainted with them. I'll be sure to include Mark Braddock. He's just returned from some Bible school in the East. I think he was studying for the mission field. You should like him for he may be your type. He's so narrow-minded and straight-laced that the girls all call him the wet blanket."

"He sounds interesting," Meredith said. "I'd like to meet him. Why haven't I seen him at church?"

"I don't think he's been there since he came home. He has a group of children over on the other side of town in some sort of mission he's starting. Since he's been off to school he's gotten too many queer ideas to work with us. I've heard

34

that he calls Rev. Hawthorne a modernist.''

Meredith smiled to herself. This young Mr. Braddock sounded as if he might prove interesting indeed. In him she might really find a friend with a kindred spirit. That mission sounded like music to her ears. It might solve the problem which had been facing her. She felt that she could not endure Rev. Hawthorne's sermons much longer. If she could help in this mission it might be an outlet from boredom and a chance to work for the Lord.

She looked forward with eager anticipation to the picnic.

CHAPTER 5

THOUGH MEREDITH TRIED TO FORGET the truck driver, Bill, her thoughts returned to him with a persistence which annoyed her. Why should she be so anxious to find out who he was when he had showed her so plainly that he did not want to know him? Why be interested in him when there were many other boys who were willing to be friendly? After all, he was only a truck driver and many of the other boys she had met were members of old and respected families and they were either in business with their fathers or they held positions of which they could be proud.

She had been taught that a person was not measured by his social position nor by his wealth, but by what he was in character. Many of her playmates had been children of poor families but they were being reared in the same pattern of Meredith's life and later on these same children had become her closest friends. So, as far as this young fellow was concerned, the fact that he was just a truck driver did not make any difference to her. Still, she wondered why she could not forget him. As time passed and she did not see him, instead of relegating him to other forgotten incidents and people of the past, he was an ever present provocative object of her thoughts.

She had not used her car often since she had come to Cedarville, for there was no occasion to use it, but this morning she decided to take it out and run it for a while so the battery would not lose what little charge it had left. She took the old road that she had traveled that first day. She did not make any excuse to herself as to why she took that road, but drove slowly along watching the way ahead.

A mocking bird perched upon a high branch was pouring forth liquid notes of melody. The faint sweet trill of a canary was imitated so perfectly that she turned in a surprise to see if perhaps some bird had escaped from its cage and was singing the faintly sorrowful song of a homesick little wanderer. Instead she saw the gray breast and the saucy tilt of the black tail of this imitator which stole the song of other feathered creatures. The bird tilted its head as she looked up at him and as if to rebuke her for interfering with its song, it uttered loud squeaks of protest, then flew away.

"You faker!" she called after the bird. "Why don't you sing your own songs instead of robbing others of theirs?"

As if in answer to her words, there came from a far branch the yodeling trill that belonged to the little thief, a clear sweet high-pitched song that no other bird possessed nor could imitate.

"Just like people," she commented. "Never satisfied with the talents or possessions God has given them, but always striving or yearning to possess what the other fellow has."

Presently she saw a truck coming and her heart began to beat a little faster. If this was the truck she hoped it would be, what could she do about it? She had no excuse, for there was no breakdown and she could not yell to the driver to stop and talk to her. What had she hoped for anyway?

As the truck drew nearer she recognized it and she drove more slowly, hoping that Bill would stop the truck, but he did not stop. He drove past with just a glance, such a short one that she could not even wave to him. She raised her hand to do so, but he was gone before she could. As she watched the receding truck in her mirror she saw it come to a sudden stop. Then it turned around and came back toward her. The driver drew along beside her and she stopped her car. He stopped the truck and got out. Her spirits rose as he came and stood beside the car.

She smiled and said, "How do you do?"

He did not return her smile but said seriously, "I've been hoping that I could see you again. I wanted to apologize for my rudeness. I'm sorry I acted that way. I really know better."

"You're forgiven. I won't hold it against you," she said and gave him another smile. "We all have our good and bad days and perhaps that day was one of your bad ones."

"They're all bad days," he said bitterly. "There are no good ones."

"I'm so sorry," she said sympathetically. "You've had some sorrow or something has happened to you to make you feel downhearted. I can understand how you feel. I too have had sorrow. The greatest sorrow of my life happened just a little while ago."

"You don't look as if you ever had a sorrow or care in your life," he said in surprise. "What do you know of sorrow?"

"My grandmother went to be with the Lord just a few weeks ago. She was both mother and father to me. When she went away I thought I couldn't stand it and even now, there are times when it seems almost more than I can bear, for I miss her so."

"Do you call that tragedy?" he asked almost gruffly.

"It is to me," she said. There was a hurt look in her eyes. "My mother went to be with the Lord when I was just a baby and I can't remember her at all. Granny was as wonderful as any mother could ever have been."

"Why do you say that they went to be with the Lord?" he asked. "Why don't you just say that they died and that was the end of them?"

"Because that wasn't the end of them," she answered quickly. "Granny's dear little worn out body died, but the real Granny that I loved never will die. She is with the Lord today in heaven and I know that one day I shall be there with her. That is why I can bear the parting now, for I know that it will not last forever."

His eyes regarded her silently and she saw curiosity and appraisal and something else in them which she could not understand.

"Do you really believe in such drivel?" he finally asked. "How can you?"

"Because it's in the Bible and I believe every word in it," she said. "The Bible is the Word of God and every word in it in the original language was inspired of Him. If you could only believe that, then perhaps you wouldn't always be so bitter and so unhappy."

"Wouldn't do me much good if I did believe it," he exploded still more bitterly. "I believe that when we die, we die, and that is the end."

"That isn't true, no matter if you do believe it," she told him. "Your body may die, but that isn't the end, for you have a soul and a spirit. The real you isn't your body, but the soul of you which makes you what you are in character and in your attitude to the world around you. Your spirit is that part of you which enables you to reach out and pray to God for forgiveness and to talk to Him when you have received Christ as your Saviour."

Why was she talking to this stranger like this? She had never talked this way to anyone on such short acquaintance. She had been careful not to force her witness upon anyone. Somehow she felt impelled to talk this way now, for the words seemed to come forth from her spontaneously.

"You really believe this, don't you?" he remarked as his eyes lingered on her.

She saw the unmistakable gleam of admiration in them this time, but that neither disturbed her nor pleased her. She had her mind intent upon something far more important just now.

"I believe it with all my soul," she said fervently. "If I didn't, I don't know how I could go on. If the Lord did not bring peace to my heart, I don't know how I could stand the ache in my heart. But He does. That is why all the days are not bad ones." Again she gave him a smile, this time a radiant one.

"I wonder," he breathed, scarce above a whisper. "Is that what makes you seem so happy and smile so easily?"

"I don't just seem happy. I am, in spite of heartache and missing my old home and my grandmother."

"You are so beautiful," he murmured, as if he were scarcely conscious that he spoke aloud.

She ignored the compliment though it stirred a little flutter in her heart, for his words were no mere idle flattery. But she was intent upon something far more important than compliments.

"If you could have the peace in your heart that I have in mine, all of your days would not be bad," she offered somewhat shyly.

"You don't know what you're saying," he said as the harsh note returned to his voice and the hard light to his eyes. "There can never be anything but bad days for me. It would take a miracle from your God to change my life and I don't believe in miracles. I once hoped for one, but it never came."

"But the God I worship is able to perform miracles," she insisted. "He could change your life if you would only give Him a chance."

"That I would like to see," he cried skeptically.

"That I would like to have you see," she echoed. "I do so want to help you. Just give God the chance to show you that He is able."

"I don't even believe that there is a God," he said and turned away.

"Oh, please don't go like this!" she cried. "Please tell me your name. I really do want to help you."

He turned upon her almost fiercely and ejaculated, "My name doesn't matter. No one can help me, so don't bother to try." Then more contritely, "Forgive me for again being rude. I do thank you for your interest, but there is nothing you or anyone else can do to make the bad days good ones."

He got into the truck and sped down the road. She watched him turn the truck around and then he passed her so swiftly that she just caught a glimpse of him with his eyes fastened upon the road ahead.

She turned her car around and drove slowly back toward town. The mocking bird was calling with shrill sharp cries to some answering bird in the distance, but she did not even seem to hear. There in the distance, now almost out of sight, was a lost soul, someone who needed the peace and abiding joy that the world cannot give or take away. And she hadn't been able to give him one word that would help raise him out of the darkness which enveloped his life.

As she rode along she prayed fervently that in some way she might be able to win that soul for the Lord. She did not realize that, deep down beneath that yearning over a lost soul, was the inexplicable interest she had in a young man with handsome face and eyes that could be so attractive if that hard bitter light could only give way to warm friendliness and to the joy that should be shining forth from them.

CHAPTER 6

THE EVENING OF THE PICNIC which Mrs. Barton had planned for Meredith was a perfect one for such an outing. A full moon hung over the lake, gleaming with a radiance that touched the dark waters with the magic of its light, turning the wavelets to silver ripples as they washed the edge of the white sands on the beach and sank into their place again with soft swishing sounds.

A bonfire had been kindled on the beach where marshmallows would be toasted later on when the group had eaten the delicious food that was spread on white cloths on low tables under the trees nearby.

The group was not large, for Mrs. Barton wanted Meredith to get better acquainted with her guests and this would not be possible if there were too many. There were fifteen invited, seven girls and eight boys. They began laughing and chattering as they greeted one another and gathered about the tables. This was a new experience for most of them, for they felt that they had passed beyond the age of marshmallow roasts. But Mrs. Barton's invitation could not be refused, for they knew that when she planned a social affair, it would be something quite special.

They were not disappointed, for the food was really "out of this world," as the girls remarked when they began to eat. A caterer had prepared everything and there were surprises galore in sandwiches, salads and cookies.

Meredith found herself paired with Mark Braddock. She noticed that Terry had come alone and she thought that he would be her partner for the evening. She was glad when one of the other girls appropriated him at once in such an unmistakable way that he could not get away from her. This girl, Cora Jones, had been decidedly cool and almost rude to Meredith from the first. Meredith understood the reason when she saw Cora's adoring gaze fastened upon Terry, and her efforts to charm him. It was a relief to her not to have Terry hovering over her all evening. Now, perhaps, those other boys would see that she did not belong to Terry and they would become more friendly. She was so used to having boys around her, willing to just be friends, that she could not help but feel isolated in the situation in which she found herself here in Cedarville.

When Mark Braddock arrived a little later than the others, Mrs. Barton took him over and introduced him to Meredith. As she acknowledged the introduction, Meredith could see the significant looks which passed between the girls near her. She thought she understood. This boy was to be her partner for the evening and they were feeling sorry for her. She remembered what they called him, the kill-joy and the wet blanket.

He certainly was not handsome. Every boy in the group was much better looking than he was. She could understand why the girls did not run after him. She wondered if he was as uninteresting as he looked.

When they sat down to eat he had little to say at first and she was forced to carry the burden of the conversation. This did not matter while they ate for there was such a babble of chatter and laughter that what one said did not count for much. When, however, the meal was finished and they sat around the camp fire before time for the speed boats to arrive, they sat a little apart from the others. It was then that she realized that Mark Braddock had something infinitely more valuable than good looks.

"Your aunt tells me that you have had the recent loss of a loved one," he remarked.

"Yes, my grandmother went to be with the Lord just a little while ago," she replied.

He gave her a warm smile that seemed to transform him and make him almost good-looking. Something glowed within his eyes there in the firelight that brought a responsive warmth to her. It was a light which she had not seen in anyone's eyes since she had left Wayne, her home town.

"You really know the Lord, don't you?" he remarked as his eyes and his lips continued to smile.

She remembered what she had said about her grandmother's death. She had used that phrase unconsciously, just as she had with Bill on the roadside.

"You mean the way I spoke of Granny's death?" she asked. "Yes, I know Christ as my Saviour, if that is what you mean."

"Now I know why I was fortunate enough to be your partner for tonight. At first I thought it was just because none of the other girls cared to be with me and because I came late, but now I can understand. At first I thought I wouldn't come, because I really don't enjoy being a wet blanket and I am, always. But how glad I am that I came."

"I'm afraid I belong in that category also," she said. "I don't do many of the things that the other girls and boys enjoy. I'm afraid they don't like me much and I have been lonely. It was so different at home. There was such a wonderful group of Christian young people who loved the things that I love and we had such good times together. We were all happy because we were doing things that counted for eternity as well as having a lot of fun."

"These young people think they are having fun," he remarked. "But fun and real joy and happiness can be far apart."

As they talked, she forgot how plain he was. There was a beauty of character that shone from his face and was evident in what he said that made him far more attractive than mere good looks. She could not help but compare him with Terry. Terry and Cora sat not far away and she caught his eyes fastened upon her more than once. She could see, even in the flickering firelight, how dissatisfied he was, for he was paying scant attention to what Cora was saying, while she exerted all her little artifices to keep him interested. Terry was quite good-looking, but there was a certain hardness about him with his self-assurance and his confidence in his power to attract that repelled her instead of making her admire his good looks. This boy who sat by her had a strength of character in his face which spoke of something more profound than mere seeking after the satisfying of the desire of pleasure. He had a purpose in life and it somehow set him apart from the others and made him someone special in her eyes. She wanted him for a friend and she felt sure that he would be.

Presently the speed boats arrived and the chattering group got in and started on the ride around the lake. Each boat held four people and the boatman. Meredith saw, with a smile of amusement, how Terry maneuvered to be in the boat she and Mark were in. She could see that Cora did not like the arrangement, but there was nothing she could do but accept as graciously as possible.

"I haven't had a word with you all evening," Terry whispered as he sat down beside her, forcing Mark to take the seat beside Cora.

"Terry!" cried Cora, unable to hide her anger at being forced to ride beside Mark. "You belong here by me. I'm sure that Meredith wants to be with Mark."

"Did she say so?" Terry asked provocatively. "If she says she doesn't want to sit with me, I shall have to move. What do you say, Meredith? Are you going to tell me to move?"

Meredith laughed to hide her embarrassment. "Of course not. What difference does it make where we sit? We're together and we're here to enjoy the ride."

Cora was reduced to a pouting silence as the motor started and the boat sped over the water, seeming to scarcely touch it. They rode on still more swiftly while the girls uttered little shrieks as the spray splashed over them and they bounced like a cockle shell over the waves.

There were other boats out racing at top speed and some of them came dangerously near their boat as they dashed by.

"It looks as if some of them are trying to hit us," Cora remarked as one came so near that they almost touched as they passed.

"It's a trick," the man at the wheel said over his

shoulder. "These speed demons enjoy scaring people by seeing how near they can come without actually hitting them. Sometime one of them is really going to hit someone and then there'll be trouble."

One after another of the boats passed them, coming too near for comfort and splashing them with spray. Suddenly from out of nowhere a larger boat tore down upon them, coming straight for them. It did not swerve as it came nearer and the man at the wheel called out,

"What's the matter with you? Are you drunk, you crazy idiot!"

There was no answer only a loud laugh. Then it struck as it sped past, a glancing blow that shattered one side of the boat the four were in. It gave a sudden lurch, then turned over, throwing everyone into the water.

"Help! I can't swim!" Cora shrieked as the boat upset.

Meredith saw Cora go down just as something struck her on the side of her head, almost stunning her. She went under but she did not lose her presence of mind. She had seen where Cora had gone under and she kicked off her slippers as she went under and swam toward the spot.

She grabbed Cora's skirt and pulled her to the surface. As they came up, Cora, gasping and with a mouth half filled with water, got a strangle hold about Meredith's neck and they both went down again.

Although she was hampered by her clothing, Meredith had strength as well as skill and she treaded water frantically until they came to the surface again. Then she did the only thing she could do, the thing she had been taught in her life saving course. She gave Cora a stiff blow on her chin. Immediately the girl's frantic clutch was loosened and she was a limp, dead weight in Meredith's arms. Turning on her side, she managed to hold Cora's head above water while she swam toward the boat which was approaching.

Hands reached out and took the unconscious Cora aboard, then they dragged Meredith in. She was too spent by the strain to say anything. She lay panting and exhausted in the boat as it turned and sped back toward the dock.

"Are the others all right?" she asked as they helped her

out and took her to where Mrs. Barton waited. Her aunt was crying hysterically.

"My poor child!" she wailed. "What a horrible end to such a happy night! I thought you were drowned. Are you all right? Are you?" she babbled, holding Meredith in her arms, heedless of her soaked clothes.

"Yes, I'm all right. Just let me sit down," Meredith panted. "Are the boys all right?" she asked again.

"Yes, they are over there. Terry got hit on the head and Mark has a badly sprained ankle, but they made it all right. There was another boat right behind yours that picked them up. They couldn't find you and they thought you were drowned."

Some of the group were taking care of Cora and presently Meredith wobbled over to where she was. Finally Cora sat up and when she saw Meredith, fire shone from her eyes.

"You hit me!" she cried. "What were you trying to do? Drown me so that you could have Terry?"

"I was trying to save your life," Meredith answered quietly. "If I hadn't knocked you out, we would both have been drowned. It was the only way to save us both."

"Cora!" one of the girls cried. "You ought to be ashamed of yourself. Meredith saved your life and you should be thanking her instead of abusing her."

"I'm sorry," Cora said, ashamed of her words and of being rebuked before them all. "Thank you, Meredith. I didn't understand. I am grateful."

Meredith wondered as she turned away and sat down if Cora was really grateful. The strain had unnerved her more than she realized. It had been some time since she had been swimming and her muscles were not used to the strain.

Terry insisted upon taking her home in his car and she did not have the energy to refuse. Just to get home and lie down was all that mattered. They drove for a little while in silence, then she began to react from the strain. Her head fell limply back upon the seat and she leaned against him, only half conscious. He looked down into her pale face, so lovely, even with the hair all wet and clinging closely to her still wet face and he could not resist the temptation to put his arm around her and draw her to him so that her head rested upon his shoulder.

He feared her rebuke, but she was too weak and shaken and too nearly unconscious to object.

He bent his head and kissed her on her cheek.

"My darling, how wonderful you were!" he murmured. "No one but you would have risked her life to save that ungrateful girl."

She did not resist his caress. Her head rested quietly upon his shoulder. It was as if she were content to let it remain there, and he felt that was where it belonged. But Meredith did not even know it was there. She was fast asleep, utterly spent from shock and exhaustion.

Presently Terry saw that she was asleep and probably hadn't heard what he had said. He was not disappointed, just content to have her in his arms. One day, before long, her head would rest there again. He was sure of that. And when that happened, she would know it was there and she would be content to let it remain there, for she would belong to him.

CHAPTER 7

THE NEXT MORNING MEREDITH WAKENED refreshed and fully recovered. She remembered with embarrassment that she had fallen asleep with her head on Terry's shoulder. He had had to waken her when they reached home. She apologized for what she had done, but she was only half awake and she scarcely remembered what he had said when he told her good night. She had a dim memory of the tone of his voice and the ardent look in his eyes as he helped her out of the car and left her with her aunt who was waiting for them on the porch. He had taken the longer way back and had driven slowly for he wanted to make the most of this opportunity to have her in his arms. Meredith vaguely remembered taking off her wet clothes with her aunt's help and sinking at once back to sleep as soon as she got into bed.

She was worried about Terry. She hoped she had not given him any false ideas about her feeling toward him. He was becoming more of a problem each day. He made no secret of his intentions toward her even though he had never said a word to her. She could see it in his every glance, in his persistent attentions, in the touch of his hand as it lingered on hers. She did not know how to cope with the situation. She could not refuse to see him again, for she had no excuse to offer when he asked for a date and she couldn't just tell him that she didn't want to go out with him, for he had been attentive and friendly in the days when she was so utterly lonely and homesick. She hoped that something would happen to enable her to gradually break off a relationship which she felt was unfair to Terry and distasteful to her. She did not want to let him go on in the hope that one day she would fall in love with him, for she knew that she never would, yet she could not tell him that when he had never said a word to her about how he felt.

Mark Braddock offered a hope for the solution of her problem.

When she came down to breakfast, her aunt greeted her with a pleased smile.

"I'm glad to see that you're all right, dear. Are you sure that you shouldn't have stayed in bed today and rested?"

"No indeed, Auntie," she replied as she kissed her and greeted her uncle. "I'm as fit as a fiddle. I was just knocked out for a while last night. If I had been in first class shape I would never have felt the experience at all, but it's been so long since I was in swimming that I wasn't up to par."

"You've had two phone calls already," Mrs. Barton told her. "Your friends are all anxious about you. Mark Braddock almost got me out of bed and just a little while later Terry called. Both of them were so concerned about you. You're a heroine now, my dear," and she gave Meredith a fond look. "Your name will be in the paper and you'll be a marked young lady from now on."

Oh, I don't want that!" Meredith exclaimed. "I didn't do anything to merit that kind of publicity. Besides, I don't like that sort of thing."

"You saved a girl's life, my dear," her aunt reminded her. "And I happen to know that that particular girl has never been too nice to you. I would never have invited her if her mother hadn't been such a close friend."

"I didn't do any more than anyone else would have done in my place," Meredith said.

"I just wonder if Cora would have risked her life for you if you had been drowning," Mrs. Barton remarked. "She was pretty catty last night."

"I didn't mind that," Meredith said. "She was over-wrought and besides, she's in love with Terry and he has been paying too much attention to me. Perhaps I'd be jealous of her if the situation were reversed."

"Meaning, I suppose, that you're not in love with

Terry," Mrs. Barton remarked.

Meredith turned to her uncle and smiled roguishly.

"Uncle William, can't you think of something to talk about to get me out of this spot? If you don't, Auntie will put me through the third degree about my love life and I can't take it this morning."

Mr. Barton smiled understandingly. "Your Aunt Mary enjoys nothing better than playing cupid, but sometimes her efforts backfire on her and she finds herself in the midst of trouble. Let's have some more hot cakes, if you don't mind, Mary, and let's talk about the weather. It looks like a good day for the ball game. How would you like to go, Meredith? It's only two of the high school teams, but they put on a good game and knowing the local boys makes it more interesting."

"I'd love to go," Meredith replied while Mrs. Barton, sufficiently silenced, rang the bell for the maid.

After breakfast Meredith phoned Mark and thanked him for asking about her. When she assured him that she was as well as ever, he asked her if he might come around in the afternoon to see her.

"I'm sorry," she said, "but I've already told my uncle that I would go to the ball game with him."

"Tell him to come along and go with us," Mr. Barton called to her, "whoever he is. That is, if he doesn't object to having an old man making a threesome."

"Uncle William says he'd be glad to have you join us if you care to."

"I'd be glad to," Mark told her.

"Well, which one was it?" her uncle asked when she hung up.

"I thought you knew," she said. "It was Mark Braddock."

"Dear me!" Mrs. Barton exclaimed. "What a dull time you'll have with him."

Mr. Barton turned to her with a twinkle in his eye.

"She'll be with me, my dear, so how could she have such a dull time? I'm glad it's to be Mark instead of that Terry fellow. All I've ever seen him do is ogle some girl and pay her silly compliments. I think this young Braddock has some sense even if he doesn't have good looks.''

"I'm sure I won't have a dull time," Meredith said. "I love a good ball game played by youngsters who are not out for money, but for the fun of it. I don't think my two escorts will bore me too much."

Later, when she phoned Terry to thank him, she was glad she had phoned Mark first. Terry asked to take her out to the club for lunch. He had the afternoon off, he explained, and wanted to spend it with her. When she told him of her previous engagement he did not conceal his disappointment and his displeasure.

"You can break the engagement," he insisted. "I'm sure your uncle will understand. He may be glad you're not going with him. Girls can sometimes be a bother to a ball fan. They ask such stupid questions just when the game's at its most exciting peak."

"Thanks for the compliment, but it so happens that I know the game well enough not to ask stupid questions. You see, I've umpired many a high school game and I know all the plays as well as the rules. I'm sure I won't be a bore to Uncle William. Besides, Mark Braddock is going with us. Perhaps he can keep me from being a bore."

"Mark Braddock!" he exclaimed in surprise, ignoring her sarcasm. "How did that happen?" There was anger in his voice.

"It was quite simple. He wanted to come over this afternoon, but I had already promised to go with Uncle William, so Uncle invited Mark to go with us. You have no cause to be angry, Terry. There will be other days when you have an afternoon off."

She was glad that this had happened. Perhaps this would be a way out, with Terry. But she did not know Terry.

Meredith enjoyed the afternoon even more than she had anticipated. The game was good, for both teams were well-matched and the score was tied until the end of the last inning. Her uncle was full of dry humor and she found that Mark could appreciate it as well as to add some of his own. Mark talked just enough and always at the right time and both she and her uncle were glad that he had come with them.

When they reached home, Mr. Barton insisted that Mark should come in and join them for dinner.

It was not until he was ready to leave that Mark was alone with Meredith. He had explained that he had a boy's club meeting at his little mission that evening. Meredith followed him to the porch.

"This had been such a wonderful day," he told her. "I have enjoyed every minute of it. I'm grateful to you and your uncle for inviting me."

"I've enjoyed it too," Meredith replied. "Those youngsters could really play. It was good to have you stay for dinner with us."

"It has meant more to me than you perhaps realize," he told her, while his eyes met hers seriously. "It means so much to find someone like you, someone with whom I can have real fellowship. I hope that I may come again soon. I'm rather lonely, for I have no family and since I came home from college with my changed views about spiritual matters, the people at the church have not been too friendly."

"I know how you feel," she said. "It's good to have you for a friend. I shall be glad to have you call when you have time."

He smiled the smile which seemed to transform his plain face.

"How about tomorrow?"

She told him he could come and they parted. She watched his tall form as he strode down the street. What a difference between the two men! No girl would ever be completely happy with Terry, for he had a roving eye and he would probably never be true for long to any girl, not even if she were his wife. Mark would not only give his whole heart to the girl who won his love, but he would spend his life trying to make her happy. And if she were the right kind of girl, they could both be so happy in the work of the Lord. She knew definitely, as she watched him disappear, that she could never be that girl. No matter how much she might respect and like him, no matter how happy he would try to make her, she could never love him.

What was the matter with her, she wondered. Would she never fall in love with anyone? Was she destined to live out her life without love and marriage and children? She had had many opportunities to marry, but for some reason which she could not understand, she had never really been in love. She had had her spurts of "puppy" love and girlish crushes, but they had lasted such a short time that they were not worth considering. And that early teen-age crush was not real love, not the abiding love which binds two lives together for life.

As she turned back within the house the memory of a handsome face, set and stern, and of two dark eyes clouded with wretchedness and hopelessness, came to her. Why did this man's face have to come to her at this moment, she thought, irritated that it should. Why should she even remember him at all? He did not even believe in the Lord she loved and there was deep tragedy in his life, a tragedy that would possibly becloud any girl foolish enough to fall in love with him. How could anyone as hard and bitter as he seemed to be, fall in love with anyone and if such a thing should happen, how could any girl ever hope to be happy with such a man?

She shut the door with a bang and went in to join her uncle and aunt in the living room.

Miles from town, a young truck driver, embittered by an unjust fate, stood looking out into the gathering darkness and from that darkness a girl's lovely face seemed to appear. Two eyes filled with compassion seemed to look into his as her lips whispered words which he had heard in the long ago and which he had buried beneath the burden of his tragedy and hopelessness. Two lips smiled at him seeking his friendship, and eager to impart the peace which their owner professed to possess. His heart stirred for a moment and the longing to see her again stole over him, but suddenly he turned away and covered his face with his hands.

"You fool!" he said to himself. "Forget her! She's not for you. What right do you have to even remember how lovely she is? What right have you to even think of her? How she would laugh if she knew the truth about you and what you feel when you think of her!"

CHAPTER 8

TRUE TO MRS. BARTON'S PREDICTION and much to Meredith's annoyance, she became a local celebrity. The story of her heroic rescue was given headlines in the local paper, together with a photograph of her and of the girl she had saved from drowning. Meredith didn't know anything about the photograph until she saw it in the paper. Mrs. Barton had given it to the reporter.

"I wish you hadn't done that," Meredith told her aunt when she saw the picture.

"Why not?" Mrs. Barton asked. "You deserve all the praise and publicity. That was a mighty brave thing you did and I'm proud of you. I think you ought to get a Medal or something for saving Cora."

"But I don't want any publicity, Auntie," Meredith replied. "I didn't do it to be a heroine or to show how brave I was. I did it almost without thinking. There was no time to think. I just knew that if I didn't do something quickly, Cora would drown. That's all there was to it and I wish people wouldn't make such a fuss over it."

The phone had been ringing all morning while Mrs. Barton beamed and Meredith grew more annoyed.

"I notice that Cora was only too glad to get her picture in the paper, even if it did give you all the praise. And I haven't seen her or heard from her since you saved her life," her aunt remarked.

"I think I know how she feels. Poor girl! She's so much in love with Terry and she thinks that what I did threw the limelight on me and made her chances of winning him even more slim than they were."

"If she had any sense, she would have seen before now that he is in love with you. He hasn't even looked at another girl since he met you."

"I wish that he would look at someone else," Meredith said with a sigh.

"Don't you like Terry?" Mrs. Barton asked in disappointed tones. "I was hoping you would. He's a fine young man and a good catch for any girl."

Meredith smiled. "I'm not out to catch anyone, Auntie. I like Terry, but I don't love him. If he would fall in love with Cora or someone else, it would make it much easier for me. He's too possessive. I don't want to be rude, for he has been wonderful to me, but I don't want to give him any false hopes. I'm sure that I'll never fall in love with him."

"I do hope you're not falling in love with Mark Braddock," her aunt remarked disdainfully. "He has nothing to offer any girl. I don't see how you can be interested in him."

"I see much in him," Meredith said seriously. "He is one of the finest young men I've met since I came here. He's a Christian in the real sense of the word and we have much in common. I'm not in love with him and I don't think I could ever be, but I do want him for a friend."

"H'm! It looks to me as if you're going to be so particular that you'll end by being an old maid."

"There are worse things that could happen to me," Meredith replied.

The ringing of the phone brought an end to the conversation and Meredith was thankful for the interruption.

Mark came often and though Mrs. Barton was hospitable and polite, Meredith could sense her dislike. The more she saw of him, the more she admired him and when she learned the story of his life, it wakened a sympathy for him while her admiration increased.

Mark had grown up in a local orphanage. His parents had been killed in an accident when he was a baby. His ambition had been to become a lawyer and after his graduation he had spent a year studying law, working his way through school. At the end of that year he had had an experience during a revival and the whole course of his life had been changed. Now he was waiting to be accepted by one of the mission boards for work in Africa, but while waiting he had not been idle. He had started a mission Sunday school and this had grown into a church.

He did not tell the story until Meredith had urged him to do so, for he did not enjoy talking about himself. How different this was from Terry! Terry enjoyed nothing better than to talk about himself and his ambitions and plans for what he would do when he finished law school.

"What branch of law were you interested in?" Meredith asked Mark.

"Criminal law," he told her. "I also had ambitions to be a criminal investigator, a sort of Sherlock Holmes, doing my own detective work along with my practice. Quite an unusual ambition, I'll admit. But when the Lord took my life over, I saw it was much more wonderful to save men's souls than to condemn men to death or to try to reform lives already given over to sin."

Terry was no more pleased over Meredith's interest in Mark than Mrs. Barton was. It seemed that too often when he phoned her for a date, she had already promised Mark.

"I wonder if you really do have a date with him," he said one day when this had happened twice in succession.

"Is there any reason why I should lie to you?" she asked indignantly.

"I'm sorry I said that," he apologized. "That's one thing I admire about you. You always tell the truth. But I can't understand why that fellow's always ahead of me when I want to get a date with you. What can you see in that dud, anyway?"

"You wouldn't understand if I should tell you," she informed him coolly.

"I suppose it's because he has none of the vices that I have, of which you disapprove," he said sarcastically, angry and jealous.

"I've never told you that you had any vices, have I?" she asked.

"No, you haven't but I know you disapprove, just the same. Cocktails and smoking, dancing and cards, and almost everything that goes to make life enjoyable are taboo with you."

"Then why bother about me if I'm such a kill-joy?"

"You know why, as well as if I told you every time I see you," he said. "If you'd only try, perhaps you could make me see things the way you do," he added with a note of pleading. "Give me a chance, Meredith. Don't put me off like this, no matter how interesting you find this other fellow."

"Can I help it if he dated me before you phoned?" she asked. "I've given you many chances, Terry, but you're not the least bit interested in my viewpoint. At least not until now."

"Are you falling in love with that fellow?" he asked. "I believe you are."

"You don't even know what love is, Terry," she flashed back. "I'm not falling in love with him or with anyone else, so let's just continue to be friends and don't be angry because I can't see you every time you phone me."

"Terry's getting worried about Mark, isn't he?" Mrs. Barton asked when Meredith had hung up.

Meredith shook a finger at her. "No fair eavesdropping."

"I couldn't help hearing," her aunt replied with a laugh. "You're going to have trouble with that young man before you get rid of him, mark my word."

"I'm not trying to get rid of him. I'm just trying to make him understand how I feel about him."

A frown wrinkled Meredith's brow. She wished she knew just how to handle Terry. Her aunt's prediction might prove true, for Terry was a most determined young man. She hoped she wouldn't have any trouble. If she could only have seen into the future, that little frown upon her brow would have grown deeper. How terribly true her aunt's predictions proved! Mercifully she was denied a peep into the future.

Mrs. Barton came to her one morning while she was in her room reading.

"I wonder if you'd do something for me, my dear," she said.

"Of course, Auntie. What do you want me to do?"

"Old Mrs. Field is home from the hospital and I promised to take her some things this afternoon, but I have a meeting to attend and I know she'll be disappointed if I don't get there. Would you mind going for me? You'll have to take your car, for I'll need mine."

Meredith was glad of the opportunity to visit the old lady. Mrs. Field was one of the few church members who believed what Meredith believed and though she had not had many opportunities to talk to her, she looked forward to the visit.

Mrs. Field lived out on the old road, several miles from town. As Meredith drove along she was thinking about the old lady, sick and alone. She drew near the spot where she had had the flat tire and once more she remembered Bill. So much had happened since she had last seen him that she had almost forgotten how anxious she had been to find out who he was and why he was so bitter, even though he still persisted in her thoughts in most unexpected ways.

She spent an hour or so talking with Mrs. Field. The old lady was glad to see her. She was lonely, for she had few visitors. She reminded Meredith so much of her grandmother that the ache in her heart and the longing for her was renewed and she almost wished that she hadn't come. As she prepared to leave, Mrs. Field said something that brought the tears to Meredith's eyes but which shed a warm glow through her heart.

"It won't be long now until I shall be able to get acquainted with your grandmother. I shall tell her how we talked about her and how much you miss her. She'll be glad to know, if she doesn't already know, that you are remaining faithful to your Lord."

Meredith looked at her silently, too touched and too near tears to say a word.

"I have only a few months longer here and I'm not sorry. The doctors say that it may be less time than that. It will be so wonderful to be there with those who have gone on before. I shall be impatient for that day to come."

"You make heaven seem more real than ever," Meredith murmured, her eyes tear-drenched.

"It's just on the other side of the door," Mrs. Field said with a smile, "and it's just as real as this old earth."

She reached up and patted Meredith's wet cheek.

"You're a dear, sweet child," she said. "I feel that the Lord is going to use you in a great way for Him. Come and see me whenever you can. If I go before I see you again, just rejoice with me."

"I'll come again real soon," Meredith promised.

Tears were still wet upon her cheek when she came upon Bill standing beside the truck, staring down at it ruefully. She stopped her car and saw that the hood of the truck was raised and that he had been trying to work on the motor. His hands were dirty and he had a smudge of grease on his face.

"You're having trouble, I see," she remarked.

"Yes. This old wreck refuses to run and I can't find the trouble. I'll have to get to the garage mechanic in town and see what he can do."

"Could I give you a lift?" she offered. "I'd be glad to take you to the garage. There is no phone near here and it's a long way to town."

"Thanks, but I can't ride with you," he said.

The brief friendly gleam in his eyes vanished and that same cloud descended over them again.

"Is there any law against it?" she asked. "I was only trying to be of help. You helped me when I was in trouble. I'd like to return your kindness."

There was hurt in her voice and he hastened to explain.

"I'm too dirty to ride with you," he said lamely. Then he saw the tears upon her lashes and still wet upon her cheek. "You've been crying!" he exclaimed in distress. "Who has made you cry?"

His voice and the look in his eyes stirred her heart to quicker beating. She dashed the tears from her eyes and wiped her cheek with the back of her hand as she smiled tremulously.

"I've been talking to a dear old lady who has only a

short time to live. She made heaven seem even more real to me than it ever was before. She longs to go there. She will soon meet my grandmother there. How wonderful it is to know the way ahead."

His eyes clouded again and he turned away.

"Perhaps, for those who believe that myth," he said dully. "My mother used to talk that way and I used to think that she knew what she was talking about. But now I know better. There is no God and there is no justice, only power in the hands of those who control what they call justice."

"Someone must have hurt you terribly to make you feel like that," she said. "How I wish I could restore your faith in what your mother believed! It would take away that unhappiness and give you peace."

"You don't know what you're saying," he said. "No one can give me peace and nothing can change what I feel. It would take a miracle and miracles just don't happen."

They had both forgotten the damaged truck until he looked down at his hands and saw how dirty they were. Then she also remembered.

"Won't you let me drive you to the garage? I won't mind the dirt and this old car can't be hurt by it."

"Thanks again," he said, "but I can't leave the truck. If you will phone the garage when you get home, I'll appreciate it."

He gave her the name of the garage. It was on her way home and she told him that she would stop there and save time. He thanked her and she drove away, leaving him standing there looking after her.

What had happened to embitter him so completely, Meredith wondered as she drove along. She thought she had found the reason why he would not ride with her when she reached the garage. She gave the mechanic the message and he said he would go at once to see what the trouble was. As he turned away she heard what he said to one of the others.

"Why don't those politicians spend a little money for some new prison trucks? Those old wrecks are costing more for repairs than they are worth."

So Bill was driving one of the prison trucks. She should

have guessed that before now, but she had been too much interested in the driver to pay much attention to the truck. Perhaps that was why he didn't want to ride with her. But that couldn't be the reason for his bitterness. What was the answer to that, she wondered. She was afraid that she would never know.

CHAPTER 9

MEREDITH WENT TO SEE MRS. FIELD often and the old lady was delighted to have her come, but Meredith had a guilty feeling that it was not solely her interest in Mrs. Field which took her out on the old road. She hoped that she would meet Bill again and have another chance to talk to him. She didn't want him to think that she was such a snob that she would object to riding with him, no matter what his occupation was. She was deeply interested in Bill, the man who needed God. She wouldn't admit to herself that she was also interested in Bill, the handsome man who had aroused her curiosity and interest.

Meredith always enjoyed her visits with Mrs. Field, for they talked of the things so dear to their hearts and she always felt uplifted as she listened to the old lady's experiences, her testings, and the Lord's provision for all her needs.

After one of these visits she met the truck coming toward her. She saw that Bill was going to pass her and she leaned out of the car and waved to him to stop. He drew to the side of the road and got out of the truck.

"Are you in trouble again?" he asked as he came toward her.

"No. I just wanted to talk to you," and she gave him a smile.

"What about?" he asked in surprise.

"Please don't misunderstand," she said, embarrassed as she realized that he had cause to be surprised. "I just wanted you to know that I know that you drive one of the prison trucks."

"Why bother to tell me that?" he asked. "I thought you knew that," he added somewhat grimly.

She felt rebuffed, but she could not stop now. She had let herself in for this and now she would have to find a way out.

"I didn't know it until I overheard the garage man saying how terrible these old prison trucks are. And I thought that perhaps that was the reason you didn't want to ride into town with me. I — I — don't want you to think that I'm that kind of a snob. I'm not that kind of a person," she finished lamely, feeling more embarrassed as his unsmiling eyes rested upon her.

Why had she been foolish enough to stop him? What kind of a person would he think she was?

"Thanks," he said without enthusiasm.

"It doesn't make any difference what a person has," she continued nervously, "how much money he makes or what kind of a job he has. It's what a person is that really counts."

"What kind of a person do you think I am?" he asked as his brooding, clouded eyes met hers.

"I know that you are a lost soul on your way to eternity without God and I do so want to help you find Him," she flashed at him boldly.

"So what?" he emitted with a shrug. "Why bother about me?"

"Because eternity is a pretty long time and I'd rather see you spend it in heaven than in — in — " and her voice faltered.

"Than in hell. That's what you started to say, isn't it?"

"Yes," she admitted.

"Don't be afraid to say it. I know what hell is. But the only hell I believe in is the hell I'm enduring here now. I've had plenty of it in the past few years. Don't bother about me. If I have a soul, it's not worth your efforts to save it, if that's what you're thinking about."

"That is just what I am thinking about," she said. "I know you think I've been persistent in trying to make you talk to me when you showed me so plainly that you didn't want to. I've practically pursued you. I've never done this before, please believe me, but I did it for only one reason. That day you changed the tire for me I saw how terribly bitter and unhappy you were and I longed to help you. I still want to," she added.

He looked at her solemnly for a moment, then said, "Am I the first unhappy person you've ever met?"

"Of course not. I've met many, for the world is so full of unhappiness. And I've been able to lead many of them to the Lord and they have learned what real joy means. You're so hardened that it seems hopeless, but I don't give up easily. I know I can help you if you'll only give me the chance."

"No one can help me," he said harshly, "so you may as well stop trying, for it will do no good. You'd better go, for someone may pass here and see you talking to me. They might not understand."

"I'm sorry if I have offended you," she said, feeling rebuked. "I know I have been shamelessly persistent. I won't bother you again."

She reached for the starter, but he suddenly put out a hand and stopped her.

"You don't understand!" he exclaimed breathlessly. "You haven't bothered me. You can't know what it has meant to me, just to get a glimpse of you. I want to talk to you, even though I don't believe what you believe about God and eternity. But it's against the rules for any of the truck drivers to stop and talk to anyone on the road. I could lose my job if I broke the rules."

"Oh, I'm sorry!" she said. "I didn't know. I wouldn't want to cause any trouble. Forgive me. I won't do it again. I just had zeal without knowledge," she added as she started the car.

She waved a good-by and left him.

"You brainless idiot!" he cried aloud. "Why did you have to tell her that? Now she'll never want to talk to you again."

He got into the truck and started the motor.

"What good would it do if she did talk to you?" he

asked himself. "How long will it be, I wonder, before she finds out the truth?"

Meredith found out the truth not long afterwards and in a most unexpected way. When she left Bill on the roadside, she felt hurt and disappointed and thoroughly disgusted with herself. What a mess she had made of trying to win him! Why had she been so persistent? What would he think of her? She had accomplished nothing except to put herself in the wrong light. Perhaps he would think that she was only using this talk about God as a pretense. She had seen other girls use many artifices and camouflages in their shameless pursuit of some boy.

Her spirits were at a low ebb as she drove slowly along, pondering over this situation. It had been unusual from the beginning. She had met other boys before under somewhat unusual circumstances, but she had never gotten into a situation like this. She knew, long afterwards, that it was, as she said often, in the plan of God, but, like many who had gone before her, she could not see the end from the beginning and it left her wondering and dejected.

Always when she was depressed or low in spirit, she did what Granny had always done, she began to sing a song of praise. Granny had said that when she was down in the depths, just to begin praising the Lord lifted her right out and put her on the mountain top again. Meredith had found this to be true, but today she had difficulty in singing a song of praise. Then she remembered the little chorus she had been singing when she had come over this same road on her way to Cedarville. She began to hum it softly and then more loudly,

> He's able, He's able,
> I know He's able.
> I know my Lord is able
> To carry me through.

She smiled as the song poured forth from her lips. It was true. God was able to deliver. He would carry her through the depths of gloom. He was able to deliver Bill from the despair which filled his heart with such bitterness. How, she did not know and she feared that she had lost her opportunity to help him, but she still had faith to believe that God was able.

She was glad for anything that could take her mind off of her none too cheerful thoughts, so when Terry called and asked for a date, she accepted with more willingness than she would otherwise have done. Terry took her to dinner at the clubhouse on the lake. His father belonged to the club and Terry was given the privilege of dining there. It was a rather exclusive club and many a girl would have envied Meredith's opportunity of going there with Terry, but Meredith was not thrilled, she was just glad of an escape this evening from her own thoughts.

While they waited for someone to serve them, Meredith looked with interest at the others there. She knew a few and they nodded friendly greetings to her. She saw several asking about her. She could tell by the surreptitious glances in her direction. Terry observed also and it brought a smile to his lips.

"They're talking about you," he commented.

"So I noticed," she said. "I suppose I look dowdy and old-fashioned in this dress."

"They're not talking about your dress," he said as his admiring eyes rested upon her. "You're the prettiest girl in this place. Besides, you're a heroine, remember? People are still talking about what you did that night on the lake."

"I'd forgotten about that," she said truthfully. So many other things had come up to make her forget that incident.

"They haven't forgotten. Look at those fellows at that table over there. See how they're looking at you. They're not bothering about the dress. They're admiring your beauty. And see those girls — they're actually green with jealousy."

She laughed lightly. "I don't see any green-eyed look in their eyes. All I see in them is disapproval of this dress. And the boys are just curious about someone who is being discussed."

"Well, they'd better stay that way and not get any ideas," he replied. "It's hard enough now to get a date with you. I don't know what I'd do if any other admirers show up." He gave her a significant look which she ignored.

"Don't worry. If they show up they won't stay very long."

She knew why they wouldn't. It had happened at home before and it had happened since she had been here. When her new date discovered that she didn't drink cocktails and didn't dance and when she wouldn't let him kiss her good night, he just didn't show up any more. And she was satisfied. They had nothing in common. If she should be foolish enough to marry a boy like that, her life would be full of tragedy and she would regret it all the rest of her life.

While they were finishing their meal several came over from other tables. Terry was forced to introduce them to Meredith, though he wished that they had not come. Not long afterwards, one of the boys returned and asked Meredith for a dance.

"Thank you, but I don't dance," she said.

The boy's mouth flew open in surprise, then he managed to say, "Oh, I'm sorry," and left them.

Terry smiled broadly. He couldn't conceal his satisfaction.

"Didn't I tell you?" she said. "You won't be bothered by them any more this evening. You'll have me on your hands and I may be a bore."

Terry turned to her and said seriously, "You could never bore me, Meredith, even when you preach," he added with a faint smile. "I can't ask for anything better than to have you all to myself, not only this evening, but all the rest of them, all the rest of my life."

"Thank you, sir!" she said and bowed with mock gravity.

"Let's go outside and watch the wild waves roar," he suggested.

She hesitated for she felt that she knew what was coming, but she could not well refuse. Best to get it over with now, she decided. Best to let him know the truth. Then perhaps he would either stay away or there would be no more efforts to ward off what his eyes had said so many times.

They sat for a while talking, just making conversation when suddenly he turned to her and took her hand.

"Meredith, there's no use putting it off any longer," he said in tones vibrating with emotion. "You've known all along that I love you, but I was so afraid to tell you, for fear that you'd send me away and I couldn't be near you. After that first blunder I made, I was afraid to even take your hand. But I can't wait any longer. I love you as I've never loved anyone before. In fact I don't think I've ever really loved anyone before. I want to marry you, Meredith. Do you care anything for me? Please say that you do!"

She let him hold her hand while she looked into his ardent eyes and tried to choose her words carefully. She didn't want to hurt him, for she knew that he was much in earnest, but she wanted to be firm and final in her answer.

"I do care for you, Terry, a great deal, but not in the way you say you care for me. I don't love you and I'm afraid I never can. But please let's be friends. I need your friendship and I do enjoy having you for a friend, but I don't love you and I can never marry you."

"Is there anyone else? Are you in love with someone back in your home town?" he asked anxiously.

"No, there is no one," she assured him. "I'm not in love with anyone else."

Why was it, that, while the words died on her lips, the image of Bill, with smudged face and greasy hands suddenly came to her? It startled her and she resolutely wiped the vision from her with a swift motion of her hand across her eyes.

"Then if there is no one else, I shall not give up hope," he said more cheerfully. "I shall try to make you love me. I don't give up easily," he added with a warning note.

"Please don't say that, Terry," she begged. "No matter how hard you try, I'm sure that will never happen."

"Why not?" he demanded. "Am I such an unattractive person?"

She smiled at this evidence of his vanity. "No, Terry, you are quite good-looking and any girl would be proud to have you for a husband as far as looks are concerned. But you see, I expect more than good looks in the man I shall be willing to marry."

"Go on. I can take it," he said. "You're going to start preaching again."

"I'm not going to preach. I've done enough of that for one night. But, Terry, don't you see? We live in two different worlds. There is really nothing in common between us. You and I think so differently about the things which are so important to me. If we should marry, I would irritate you and you would hurt me constantly, so there could never be any real happiness in such a marriage. Before long you would be sorry that you married me and perhaps your love might even turn to hate."

"Never!" he declared as his hold upon her hand tightened. "I would love you if you preached to me every hour of every day."

"My preaching would never do any good unless it made you change your mind and heart and even your life," she said somewhat sadly.

"It might even do that," he assured her. "At least I shall not give up hope until some fellow takes you away from me. And I dare anyone to even try." He leaned nearer and said, "Won't you kiss me just once, Meredith? I've longed for your kiss so many times. Won't you grant me just that one little request?"

"No, Terry. I'm sorry, but I can't," she said as she drew away. "If I should ever fall in love with you, I would give you my lips gladly. But just now I can't. I want to save my lips for the man I love."

"That man shall be me," he said grimly. "I'm willing to wait."

She did not tell him so, but she knew that he would wait a long time and even then it would never happen.

When she returned home, she was once more depressed. She felt sorry for Terry and she was worried about herself. Why did she have to think of Bill just at that moment tonight? What was wrong with her?

Many harrowing months would pass before the answer came.

70

CHAPTER 10

MEREDITH BECAME INTERESTED IN MARK'S mission church on the other side of town. She had gone with him at first, just to encourage him in his venture, but when she arrived at the place she was surprised to see the number who came to the services.

Mark had rented a small vacant store and had made it look attractive with his limited means and the help of those in the neighborhood who had become interested. The membership was drawn from the workers in a factory on the outskirts of town. Their families lived nearby and they were glad to have a place of worship which they could attend without paying bus fare. Then too, the old established churches with their membership drawn from the families of the older and more prosperous citizens, made these people feel out of place. Under Mark's ministry many of them had accepted Christ as their Saviour.

Meredith offered to teach in the Sunday school. She visited in the neighborhood and gathered a group of boys and girls. She enjoyed the work for it was what she had done in her old home and the children loved her and were eager to learn.

She knew that this would not please her aunt and Mrs. Barton did express her disapproval, but since Meredith continued to go with her to the morning service at her church, she could find no cause for complaint. Mark's services were in the afternoon. Mrs. Barton told Meredith that she thought the work was degrading and she feared people would talk.

"You'll come in for a lot of criticism," she commented crisply.

"I don't mind their criticism," Meredith told her, "as long as I know that I'm doing something worth while for the Lord. The religious leaders criticized Jesus while He went about doing good, so why should I escape? I'm not better than He was."

Her aunt looked at her with a spark of anger in her eyes.

"Couldn't you do work for the Lord in your own church instead of going down there among those factory workers in a little old store that's ready to tumble down?"

"Your church is not my church, Auntie," Meredith reminded her. "My membership is still back in Wayne and I intend to keep it there until I see what the future holds for me. I couldn't do work in your church because they don't want me. They don't believe what I believe. Rev. Hawthorne made that quite clear to me when I attended a meeting when I first came here. He as much as said that anything that was not taught in their church literature was heresy. So, I'm a heretic in his eyes."

"You'll be in the same class as that Mark Braddock," retorted Mrs. Barton witheringly, "and you know what they think of him."

"I shall feel honored if they put me in the same class with him," Meredith retorted with spirit. "Mark is a consecrated Christian and he's doing a good work here. Before long he'll be going to those who've never had a chance to hear the Gospel. He's precious in the Lord's sight, no matter what those snobs at the church think about him."

"I do hope you're not getting any wild idea of marrying him and running off to risk your life to teach a bunch of savages who might kill you instead of listening to your preaching," Mrs. Barton said in alarm.

Meredith had to laugh at the look of horror on her aunt's face.

"No, Auntie, I don't feel called to go as a missionary. If I did, I would surely go and I am sure that the Lord would protect me. If not, there's no more glorious death than a martyr's death and I would be willing for that, even. Don't be afraid that I'll marry Mark. I've told you that I didn't love him and I don't. Perhaps, as you said, I may live out my life in single blessedness.''

Mrs. Barton disdained a reply, for which Meredith was thankful.

True to his warning, Terry proved a persistent suitor and Meredith saw that there was grim determination in his effort to win her love. He did not annoy her with any pleas for her love, but he was always there whenever he had time off and whenever she was free to give him a date. He exerted himself to be entertaining and she was forced to admit that he was. He was thoughtful and tried to antici- pate her every wish. He showered her with flowers and candy, for she had made him understand in the beginning that she would accept nothing else. She had tried to make him stop sending flowers and bringing candy but he refused to obey her request.

"That is the only way I have of making you remember me when I'm not able to be with you," he had explained.

As Mrs. Barton remarked, rather sarcastically, Mere- dith seemed to be "stuck" with just these two steady boy friends. All the others, after one or two dates, had left her severely alone. While they had admired her beauty and her personality, they could not be interested in going with her when there were so many other girls who lived life as they preferred to live it. Meredith was satisfied to have it so, for she enjoyed being with Mark and she enjoyed her work in his church. While Terry worried her at times, she did enjoy his company and since he would not take no for an answer, she continued their association, hoping that something would happen to end a situation which was sometimes a source of worry to her.

Mrs. Barton had had the cook bake a cake for Mrs. Field and Meredith offered to take it to her. The old lady loved sweets and Meredith often shared Terry's gifts of candy with her. She spent an hour or so with her and they had a happy time together.

When Meredith left, she drove along singing softly to herself. Her heart was full of joy and praise, as it always was after a visit with the old lady who was near the end of her journey and eager to enter the life beyond.

Suddenly the motor began to sputter and jerk, then the car came to a stop. She managed to pull over to the side of the road when she realized that something was wrong and there she sat, wondering what had happened and how she could get help. She got out and raised the hood and looked helplessly at the motor. She didn't have the least idea what was wrong and she knew that it wouldn't do her any good if she did, for she couldn't fix it. She slammed the hood down and got back in the car.

"How silly to even look at it," she grumbled to herself. "I couldn't do anything about it even if I knew what was wrong."

She hadn't been thinking of Bill but of the things she and Mrs. Field had been talking about, but when she saw the truck coming toward her, she uttered a sigh of relief. If he couldn't find the trouble or repair it, he could at least send help. She got out of the car and stood waiting hopefully. After their last meeting she did not have the courage to signal to him for help. She wondered if he would pass her without stopping. She gave another sigh of relief as he slowed down and brought the truck to a stop.

"In trouble again?" he asked as he came over to her.

"Yes," she said, then added apologetically, "it seems that I'm always bothering you. This time the old car just stopped and refused to go."

He raised the hood and took a look at the motor. She followed and stood beside him.

"I'm sorry to bother you. I don't want to cause you any trouble or make you lose your job. If you'll just phone the garage for me when you get to a phone, I'd appreciate it."

He turned and looked at her and his eyes became luminous with a light that filled her with amazement.

"You're not a bother," he told her in the warmest tones she had ever heard him use. "You never could be. Forget about the job. But I have my doubts about being able to find the trouble. I'm not a very good mechanic. I had my chance to learn but I wouldn't take it," he added as he turned back to inspect the motor. His voice was once more tinged with bitterness.

"We so often throw away opportunities," she commented.

He did not answer and she remained silent. She wanted to talk to him but he gave her no encouragement and she could not force her conversation upon him. She felt that she had done that too often before.

He examined the motor carefully, then went to the rear and uncapped the gas tank. He got a stick from the truck and stuck it into the tank.

"You're out of gas," he told her. "I'll have to get someone from the garage to either find the trouble or pull you in if that is not the real trouble."

"Thank you for trying and let me say that I'm sorry if I delayed you."

They did not notice the approaching car until it came to a stop nearby, then Meredith saw Terry get out and come toward them. He strode to them wrathfully.

"What's the meaning of this?" he demanded furiously. He addressed his remarks to Bill.

"This young lady had car trouble and I was trying to help her," Bill answered.

Their gaze clashed and Meredith could see that there was hate in both their hearts.

"You know the rules," Terry said. "You also know the consequences if you break them."

"Just a minute, Terry," Meredith interrupted. "Don't blame him. Blame me if you must blame anyone. Why should you be so furious because I needed help and he was kind enough to try to help me?"

"He could have sent someone to help you when he got back to the prison," Terry retorted, his eyes still blazing.

Bill stood by silently, with white face and eyes that were filled with hate. Meredith glanced at him and then turned indignantly to Terry.

"You should be ashamed of yourself, Terry!" she blazed. "What right have you to talk to him that way when all he did was to try to help me? You act as if he was some sort of criminal."

Terry smiled a cruel smile. Meredith saw Bill's startled look as his hands suddenly clenched.

"Evidently you don't know who this fellow is," Terry said. "He is a criminal and one of the worst type. He's a trusty, but he's a robber and a murderer and if I report this incident to the warden, he'll have his liberty taken away from him."

Bill raised his hand threateningly but suddenly dropped it again and stood there white and immobile as his harrowed gaze rested on Meredith's face. She glanced at him, wide-eyed and shocked, then she saw the stricken look in his eyes and heart went out to him.

She turned to Terry and said coldly, "I don't believe you," but there was no conviction in her voice.

"Thanks for the compliment," Terry remarked. "I should know, shouldn't I? This man has been in prison for over three years."

He turned to Bill and ordered him to leave.

"Get on your way. I'll see the warden about this," he warned. "You know the consequences."

Bill hesitated a moment while his hands clenched and unclenched nervously. Meredith could see that he was restraining the urge to strike Terry. Then he turned to the truck.

"If you dare tell the warden about this and make him take away that man's liberty, don't ever come near me again!" she blazed. "If you're capable of such a petty, spiteful thing as that, I don't want you for a friend."

Bill heard the wrathful words as he got into the truck and his face softened.

"Bless her!" he murmured as he started the motor. "She'd be better off if she never saw that rat again."

"Why should you be so interested in that fellow?" Terry asked. "He's not worth your sympathy."

"He is a human being and he was kind enough to try to help me," she replied, still angry and feeling sorry for Bill. "You did a spiteful thing by threatening him like that. You deliberately tried to humiliate him because you knew you could. It was cowardly of you."

"You humiliated me before that criminal when you gave me that ultimatum," he retorted, stung by her accusation.

"You deserved to be," she told him and her eyes were angry and hostile. "You could have forgotten the rules for once when you saw what he was trying to do for me."

"I only saw that he was there close beside you and I saw a look in your eyes that I've never seen when you looked at me," he confessed. "I'm jealous of any man who looks at you or anyone who is near you."

"What a happy time I would have as your wife!" she exclaimed. "You've let your jealousy make you imagine something that you didn't see."

Just what had he seen in her eyes, she wondered. Had he seen and misunderstood her ardent desire to be friends with Bill? But Terry said that Bill was a murderer. The thought filled her with horror.

"I know I shouldn't feel that way, but I just can't help it," Terry admitted. "You don't know how much I love you, Meredith."

"I know how unhappy you would make my life if I should be foolish enough to marry you," she said bitterly. "I would be afraid to even speak to another man."

"It would be different if you belonged to me," he assured her. "It's because I'm so afraid that someone will take you from me that makes me so jealous."

"Jealous of a prison trusty?" she asked witheringly.

His face flushed.

"Let's get in my car," he said. "We'll have to send the garage man out to tow your car in if he can't fix it."

"I won't go a step with you unless you promise not to speak to the warden about what happened. Will you give me your word that you won't have that man's liberty taken away from him?"

"Why do you make an issue of this?" he asked irritably.

"Because I was the cause of all of this and because I

know you hate that man. I saw it in your eyes. I repeat, if you are so vindictive toward that man that you'll use this to hurt him, I don't want anything more to do with you.''

"All right. I'll promise not to say anything about it," he said grudgingly.

They got into his car and drove for a time in silence. Terry was angry with Meredith and furious because he had lost an opportunity to vent his spite upon Bill.

"Why do you hate that man, Terry?" she asked presently.

"I don't hate him. I just dislike him. Although he's a murderer and only escaped the electric chair by a technicality, he doesn't act like a convict should."

"How should a convict act?"

He detected the sarcasm in her voice and it made him even more uncomfortable. He knew that she was angry with him but it only made him more angry over the whole affair.

"He should have some respect for those who uphold the law," he explained lamely. "That fellow doesn't. Ever since he was made a trusty his every look, even the way he obeys orders, shows his contempt for the law and those who are in authority over him."

"How did he get to be a trusty if he's such a bad character? I thought only those who had been model prisoners and merited such a concession were allowed to become trusties."

"That's true. He was a model prisoner as far as that goes. He averted a prison riot and as a reward he was made a trusty, but he made a fool out of me, for I should have known what was brewing. I got a reprimand from the sheriff and if my uncle hadn't intervened, I suppose I would have lost my job."

"That is why you hate him," she commented.

"I said I didn't hate him. Sure, I don't like him. But I was only doing my duty when I reprimanded him and reminded him that he had broken the rules. Prison rules have to be strict. Criminals are little better than savage beasts."

"They are human beings with immortal souls," she said sadly. "Some of them would not be there if they had had a chance to know a better way of life and to realize that the way of the transgressor is hard.''

"Most of them would be there, no matter what kind of chance they had. It's just born in them to be criminals. Take this Bill Gordon, the one you're championing. He had every opportunity to make good in life. He had a good position in the bank, but he couldn't be satisfied to earn a decent living. He had to steal about fifty thousand dollars and then murder his partner to keep from being found out. Do you say that he didn't have a chance to know a better way of life?''

She didn't answer him. So his name was Bill Gordon and he had stolen a fortune and murdered a man. Somehow she couldn't reconcile that story with the Bill she had come to know in their brief acquaintance.

When they had left the garage and reached her home, Terry turned to her with pleading in his eyes. His anger had disappeared and he was afraid that this would make a difference in their relationship. He was sorry that he had revealed his hatred of Bill to her. It would have been so much better if he had been diplomatic and magnanimous in her presence. He should have known what her reactions would be.

"You aren't going to be angry with me forever, because of this, are you, Meredith? Please don't let it keep me from seeing you. I can't stand it if you do.''

"If you keep your promise and try to be merciful to that prisoner,'' she said. "Isn't it better to temper justice with mercy, even while the law is being fulfilled?''

"Perhaps you are right,'' he conceded. "I shall try to remember in the future. If you've forgiven me, won't you let me come around tonight and take you for a ride? We could have a late snack at the club.''

"I'd rather not tonight, Terry. I'm tired and I want to go to bed early. Another night when you can get off.''

He caught her hand and pressed it to his lips while he murmured, "Thanks for your forgiveness, lady of my heart.'' Then more seriously, "I don't want to annoy you by telling you how much I love you, but always remember that I do.''

How she wished that he would forget, she thought as he

drove away. She didn't want to go anywhere or see anyone this evening. She wanted to be alone with her thoughts. Those thoughts and most disturbing they were, were of Bill. Bill Gordon. Now at last she knew his name. No wonder he had been ashamed to tell her. No wonder he thought she shouldn't be seen with him. No wonder he didn't want her to talk to him. He knew that others in the town knew what she didn't know about him. He knew that it would compromise her. She wondered why she hadn't guessed all along that he was a prisoner. How stupid of her!

Try as she would, she could not reconcile the two men, the Bill she had known for so short a time and the Bill Gordon Terry had pictured to her as a killer and a robber. She had had contact with other prisoners before, for she had been to the prison near Wayne many times, both for services and as a visitor now and then to someone whom she had contacted in the hospital.

Bill was not like any of these. She had seen evil and cruelty in some of these others, hardness and craftiness, but never the clear-eyed look that she had seen in Bill's eyes, even when they were also hard and bitter. Perhaps the reason for that bitterness was not that he had committed a crime. Perhaps he was innocent. So her thoughts revolved round and round until at last she went to bed and tried to sleep. But the memory of that white stricken face and those tightly clenched fists robbed her of sleep for many long hours.

CHAPTER 11

MEREDITH WAKENED THE NEXT MORNING with a feeling of depression which seemed like a great weight upon her heart, plunging her down into the valley of gloom. The morning was bright and beautiful. The sun gleamed warmly and benignly through the blinds, spreading bars of light across the room and upon the thick carpet with its pattern of gay flowers.

She sat on the side of the bed and thrust her feet into her slippers and she wondered why this feeling of depression challenged the glory of the new day. Then she remembered. Bill's white face with that look of hate, and the tightly clenched fists. She remembered Terry's hostile eyes and his harsh words of command, as if Bill were a slave or an animal who only lived to obey. She remembered what Terry had said about Bill. He was a criminal and every criminal was little better than a savage beast.

She went to the window and looked out upon the garden below where flowers were growing in profusion. The roses with their pink petals softly curved gave out their fragrant perfume. A humming bird hovered over a bush of blue bells, its brightly feathered wings whirring so fast that they made only a gray blur against the background of green and blue.

Her eyes were on the bird dipping into each flower with precision and then whirring to the next one, then darting out of sight to some nearby nest, but her thoughts were not on the bird nor the lovely garden.

Try as she might, she could not believe what Terry had said about Bill. It just didn't seem possible that Bill could be a murderer. He didn't look like a man who would rob and then murder to keep from being discovered. She laughed mirthlessly. How should a murderer look, anyway? What should there be about him to betray the fact that he had killed? She had seen pictures of men wanted for crimes, either in the paper or in the local post office and she knew that some of these men were not only young, but even good-looking.

But this, she argued to herself stubbornly, was not why she could not believe that Bill was a murderer. There was something else. She couldn't define it, but she just knew. She hoped he was not that kind of a person. She caught herself up with a start. Just why did she hope so strongly that he was not a murderer and a robber? He was a prisoner. There was no denying that. Terry had said that he had barely escaped the electric chair and there was no need for Terry to tell her that if it wasn't true. What difference should it make to her why he was there? He was still a lost soul who needed a Saviour. Her interest in him had been purely impersonal and there was no reason for her to change her mind about wishing she could help him. Now, however, there would be little chance of her ever being able to even talk to him again.

As she began to dress, an annoying thought persisted in intruding upon her. Had her interest in Bill been entirely impersonal? Had her interest in him been entirely the desire to win his soul for the Lord? She brushed the thought aside impatiently. Of course it was! How could it be anything else? A criminal! She shuddered as she hurried into her clothes and joined her aunt and uncle at the breakfast table. She wanted someone to talk to and she was glad this morning even of her aunt's continual flow of chatter while they ate.

Mark came that evening for dinner. Mrs. Barton greeted him with more warmth than usual. Now that she was convinced that Meredith would not throw herself away on this young man with his narrow-minded views about life, she was willing to receive him graciously as often as he came. She still hoped that Meredith would tire of Mark's dullness and turn to Terry who was so far more desirable as a possible husband.

Mr. Barton had grown to like Mark a great deal and

seemed to enjoy his company. He liked Mark's energy and the work he was doing, holding down a part time position during the day while he pastored his little church and looked after the needs of his members. Even though he did not share Mark's views about spiritual matters, he admired him for what he was doing. He made no secret of his dislike for Terry.

Meredith was amused by her aunt's concern over the situation when she heard her husband sounding Mark's praises. She expressed her opinion of Mark in no uncertain terms and they were not flattering.

After dinner Meredith went for a ride with Mark. She wanted to talk to him about what had happened, yet she hesitated to say anything about it. She longed to talk to someone about Bill, but she could not bring herself to talk about him, even to Mark. Perhaps he might not understand how she felt about Bill. Did she understand herself? She wondered.

Mark was talking but she did not reply to what he was saying. He turned to her and smiled quizzically.

"I don't believe you heard a word I said," he commented.

"I'm sorry. What were you saying?" she said contritely.

"I said I think I have obtained permission to have services at the prison. Remember, I told you that I was going to see if we couldn't hold services there at least twice a month. Some of the other churches hold services there, but I'm afraid they are not giving those prisoners the kind of ministry they need so much."

"When will you know?" she asked.

"In a week or so. Until now there has not been any time available but one of the other groups is discontinuing its services and I may be given that time. I think we can get some of our young people to go along with us to sing choruses, don't you?"

"I'm sure we can," she said but without enthusiasm.

"You don't sound very enthusiastic about it," he remarked. "I thought you were all for it. You thought it was a wonderful opportunity for us to win some of those prisoners for the Lord.''

"I still do," she said. "I shall be glad to help any way that I can.''

If all of those prisoners were as hardened as Bill, that would be a difficult task. But God was able. She wondered if Bill would ever come to any of those services. How strange it would be to see him in prison when she had thought of him all along as just a young man who had been embittered because life offered nothing better than driving a truck. What would it be like to see him sitting there in his prison garb and to know that he was a murderer and a robber? She shrank from the thought.

When Terry asked for a date a few days later, she could not refuse him. He took her to a little wayside inn which was noted for its chicken dinners. He sought a table in a far corner away from the few who were dining there.

"We can talk better here," he said. "This is better than the club. People are always barging in on us there.''

He did his best to entertain her and she tried to respond to his mood but she failed miserably. While he was talking, telling little amusing incidents of his college days, she could not see his animated face for the memory of the one she had seen in that encounter with Bill. She saw once more the hate-filled eyes and the stern expression as he ordered Bill to leave. She remembered his threat and the sense of gloating which she seemed to detect as he uttered it and she thought she knew what lay beneath this suave smiling exterior. Underneath all his charm there lay a vindictive, cruel nature and an unforgiving spirit which would hold a grudge and never be satisfied until that grudge had met with retaliation and vengeance. She began to feel an aversion to him which she had felt at first but which she had lost sight of while their friendship had grown. It returned now with added strength and she wondered how long she could keep him from suspecting it.

He must have sensed something in her attitude, for suddenly he stopped his gay chatter and looked at her with eyes suddenly grown serious.

"You're still angry with me, aren't you?" he asked.

"No, I'm not," she denied.

"Then why are you so silent and distant?"

"I wasn't aware that I was."

"You said you had forgiven me and I believed you," he remarked reproachfully. "You're not keeping your word and that is one of the things I have admired about you. You always mean what you say and you always keep your word."

"I do forgive you," she assured him. "You said you wouldn't have Bill punished and I believe you."

He gave her a look which made her wonder.

"Bill," he said. "You talk as if you knew him."

"You called his name yourself." She was angry at his look yet she felt guilty.

"I'd forgotten," he said as his face relaxed and he gave her a smile. "Let's forget him. We're here to enjoy ourselves, not to discuss criminals."

"No, but I want to know something. Tell me something about the crime that this Bill is in prison for. How did he happen to commit murder and how did he escape the electric chair?"

"I don't see how that fellow's crime can be of so much interest to you," he said with a trace of irritation. "He's caused me enough trouble already."

"Have you never heard of woman's curiosity?" she asked. "Is it too much trouble for you to satisfy it?"

"I may as well, or you'll never listen to anything I say if I don't. That fellow robbed a bank. He and another fellow, Fred Barker, worked in the bank. Part of their job was to close the vault after the last money was put in for the day. Bill let Barker go before closing time, even though it was against the rules, for Barker had some important engagement. Bill took this opportunity to rob the vault. It seems that this particular pile of cash was in a place where it wouldn't be missed until the bank examiner came around to check. Barker forgot something and returned to the bank in time to see Bill put the money into a brief case and start away with it.

"Bill caught sight of him as Barker was trying to hide. Later on Bill killed him and put the body in the creek about a mile from town. By the time the body was discovered it was so decomposed that it could not be positively identified as Barker's body, although it still had the remains of clothing which was identified as Barker's."

"How did they get all this information if Barker was dead?" Meredith asked.

"Barker was afraid that Bill would murder him and he wrote a letter to the police telling what had happened. He asked for police protection. He said in his letter that Bill had come to his room and threatened him. Bill was making plans to leave town on his vacation. When the police went to see Barker he had disappeared. They arrested Bill at the bus station. While they were holding him for questioning, the body was found. Because there had been some doubt about the body, the jury recommended life imprisonment. It seems that some boys found the body when they were fishing in the creek. That's the story. Now can we talk about something else?"

"Did they get the money back?" she asked while a little frown wrinkled her brow.

"No. Bill swore that he did not take the money. Of course he swore that he did not kill Barker, but the note and the body were evidence enough to convince the jury. Bill's lawyer, appointed by the court, did not seem too keen about the case. He seemed to feel that he was defending a guilty man and I think he was glad when the trial ended as it did without capital punishment. Any other cross examinations?"

"No, none," and she gave him a faint smile.

While they talked and ate their meal and then rode for a time, Meredith was thinking of Bill and the story of his crime. She found it hard to believe, even though the evidence pointed so strongly to his guilt. She knew that it was foolish to harbor such a stubborn doubt of his guilt, but it persisted, nevertheless. She wished that she could talk to Bill and hear the story from his lips. Perhaps it would be different. But of course it would, she told herself. Did she expect him to tell her that he was guilty when he had sworn that he was innocent? Perhaps she would never have another chance to talk to him and, no matter what he might tell her, there was nothing she could do about it. There was small chance that she would ever be able to win him for the Lord, so she might just as well forget the whole affair as well as Bill.

She was glad when she reached home at last. She let Terry hold her hand with a possessive tightness while he stood as close as he dared and murmured his good night. She felt that it would atone for the coldness that had crept into her feeling for him.

"I shall sleep more soundly tonight, now that I know I am forgiven," he said. His eyes looked pleadingly into hers and they told her what his lips dared not utter. "Please try to like me a little," he begged.

"I do like you, Terry," she told him. "If I did not, I wouldn't go out with you," she added.

He gave her hand a gentle squeeze and said in low tones, "I want you to like me very, very much, Meredith. I want that more than anything else in my life."

"Even more than that coveted diploma in law?" she asked.

"Please be serious," he said with a frown. "If you put it that way, the answer is yes."

"Forgive me, Terry," she said contritely. "I did not mean to be unkind. Good night and thank you for a lovely evening."

She entered the house slowly, her mind still on Bill. How could he have done such a terrible thing? What a wreck he had made of his life when he could have done so much with it! It must be true, she said to herself dolefully. He was past hope as far as she was concerned, perhaps past hope from any source. It would take a miracle to break down that wall of unbelief and to create a clean heart when it was now so blackened by sin. But God was able. She could only pray that, in some way, by some means he might have that miracle performed.

She climbed the stairs with feet that seemed like leaden weights while once more the black cloud of depression settled down upon her.

She was on her knees a long time before she got into bed.

When she finally went to sleep she had a strange dream.

She saw Bill out upon the lake in a leaky boat. As she stood on the shore watching him struggling to row the boat which was slowly sinking, she cried out to him, "Bill, get out of the boat and swim for the shore! If the boat sinks, you'll go down with it."

The boat sank lower and as he went down with it, slowly but surely into a watery grave, he held out his hands to her and cried out in an agony of entreaty, "Save me, Meredith! Save me! No one else is there to save me but you. I don't know how to swim. Save me!"

She took off her shoes and was about to plunge into the water when Terry suddenly appeared and held her back.

"You can't get to him," he said. "He's past hope. Let him die. He's no good to anyone. He's little better than a wild beast."

She wakened with a start and lay there trying to recall the horrible details of the dream, then she buried her face in the pillow and cried until at last she fell asleep again.

CHAPTER 12

SUMMER DRIFTED INTO THE PAST after one lingering hot breath and gave way to cooler but more dreary days of the fall. The season entered with chill rains and clouded skies and the whole countryside was reduced to a soggy muck of rainwashed fields and muddy roads.

In spite of rain and clouds, Meredith made her daily rounds in her work among Mark's church members. She visited the families of her pupils and helped many of them with their problems. She was able to tide some of them over their financial difficulties. She was using much of the income from her grandmother's estate to help these people as well as to help support missionaries on the foreign field. She planned to help Mark with his equipment and passage when he was ready to go. The mission board under which he was to work required at least a year of service and testing on the home field and Mark had decided to wait another six months or possibly longer, until he could find someone to take over the work he had started. He had had no idea when he had first started the Sunday school that the work would grow as it had. He told Meredith that perhaps his faith was not as strong as it should have been. They now had quite a good congregation and many souls had been won through this ministry.

Meredith was anxious to keep busy, not only for the sake of the work, but for her own peace of mind. For many days after she had heard the story of Bill's crime, she was unable to cast off the depression which seemed to weigh her down. She knew that this was not only an unhealthy mental attitude, but that it was not right for a Christian to continue in this frame of mind. One who trusted God and believed that all things worked together for good to one who loved the Lord, should look up and trust and have peace of mind and heart, instead of looking at that which would drag one down to worry and despondency. She not only prayed to forget the whole situation, as well as Bill, but she plunged into the work which she loved, with zeal and determination to be cheerful and not grieve over what she could not help.

One small worry raised its head. She knew that Mark was falling in love with her and she did not know what to do about it. He had never said a word to indicate how he felt toward her, but she knew by her feminine intuition and also by the look in his eyes which she discovered when he thought she was not noticing.

She did not want anything to come between them, for if it did, then they could not work together and her work with him was the only real joy she had known since Granny had died. She hoped that Mark would be so engrossed in his work that he would not have time to think of her as an object of his love, but it seemed that her hope and even her prayers about him were destined to prove in vain. As she thought about it afterwards, when she had seen so clearly God's promise in many events which she could not understand just now, she thought that perhaps this came as a testing and a strengthening of character to Mark. He needed every testing now, so when greater ones came on the foreign field where the forces of evil were dominant, he would have the needed strength to overcome by the Power he had learned to trust and which he knew would never fail, because he had put that Power to the test.

What she had feared and what she had tried to avoid came suddenly and unexpectedly. They had begun their services at the prison and a group of young people went with them. They sang and then before Mark gave a short but powerful gospel message which revealed God's plan of salvation and His love for every human whom He had created, some of the young people from the mission gave short testimonies.

One of these was a young boy named Dave who had recently become a member of the group. He told how he had begun a life of crime. He told his story in a boyish simplicity, but with sincerity and earnestness. He had joined a gang of teen-agers who were planning to rob a certain filling station. On that very afternoon Meredith had met him and talked to him and invited him to one of their parties at the church. He had gone with two other members of the gang, just for a lark. They had planned to break up the party and have a rowdy time, but their plans never materialized. Meredith had won their respect from the moment she greeted them and tried to make them feel welcome and they acknowledged with whispered, shamefaced remarks to one another, that they had better just stay and see what happened. If they got bored, they could walk out.

They joined in the games with half-hearted interest and just before the party ended Meredith gave them a short message. The two boys wanted to go but Dave said he wanted to stay and hear what she had to say. The others left and he remained and as Meredith talked to them about the love of God and the joy and peace that comes to those who love and follow Him, he wondered about this, for he had never heard anything like it before. He had come from a divided home where the father had been a drunkard and the mother did not know the Lord.

As Meredith spoke, she gave the contrast between a life dedicated to God and a life lived without God. This picture fitted Dave so perfectly that he thought that surely she must know all about him. He did not realize that she was being guided in her remarks by the Holy Spirit, but he knew before she finished speaking that he wanted the peace which she so beautifully presented. His own life had been a wild search for that which would satisfy and he had never found it. She made him realize where his life was leading him.

"It would have led me right here where you fellows are now," he said with boyish candor as he looked over the assembled prisoners and into their faces, many so deeply marked by sin.

He told them how, when Meredith gave the invitation,

he went forward after a struggle with himself, for he felt ashamed to acknowledge what he was before those other young people. He had looked them over while Meredith was speaking and he had intuitively felt that they had the thing she had been talking about, peace within.

She put her arm around him as he knelt by one of the chairs and talked so simply and understandingly that he could not fail to know what he must do. She said that all he had to do was to confess that he was a sinner like all of us were until the Lord Jesus forgave us and gave us a new spirit and eternal life. All he had to do was to ask the Lord to save him for Jesus' sake and then to believe that He did what He said He would.

"It seemed so easy that I couldn't believe it at first," Dave said, "but before I knew it I was asking Him and then I was blubbering like a baby. Then when I looked into her eyes and saw her smile and tell me that God has saved me, I knew it was true. I wouldn't take a million dollars for what I have in my heart now. I've got peace, fellows, and that's what you need, every last one of you."

As Meredith listened, her heart overflowed with thanksgiving. This was worth more than any joy that the world could bring, just to know that she had been allowed to win this boy for the Lord. What a privilege! What joy there would be one day when she and Granny would meet before the judgment seat of Christ! She would look at Granny and her eyes would say, "I was able to do this all because of you. You will share in my reward, whatever it may be."

She saw that there were tears in the eyes of some of the prisoners, but on the faces of the others there was nothing but the impassive unbelief and contempt of hearts hardened against the pleading of the Holy Spirit.

She caught a sudden glimpse of Mark looking at her with such adoration in his eyes that she caught her breath and turned away. She would have to hurt him and how she would hate to do that!

It was on their way home, after they had left the others, that it happened, that which she had hoped to avoid. They had told Dave how proud they were of him. Dave's eyes were glowing, for he had also seen tears in the eyes of some of the prisoners.

After they had left Dave, Mark turned to her and said in a voice husky with emotion, "That boy is a jewel of yours, my dear."

He turned his gaze back to the road and remarked in a matter-of-fact voice, "Have you ever thought of the wonderful work you could do on the mission field?"

"No, I haven't," she confessed. "I have thought about going into some full time work for the Lord and I have prayed about it, but I have not learned just what the Lord would have me do. I know definitely that I have no call for the foreign field. I'm sure that if that were God's plan for me I would know it definitely, since I am willing to go wherever He would lead me."

"Perhaps God was letting you wait so that you could go as a missionary's wife," he said as he glanced at her with a smile. "You've known for a long time that I love you, Meredith, darling," he said quietly. "Next to my Lord, I love you more than anything in life, perhaps more than my own life and I have prayed so constantly that if it was the Lord's will, you would return my love. Is there any hope for me that you could ever love me?"

He brought the car to a stop before her home and looked at her with such pleading that it brought the tears to her eyes.

"Mark, I'm sorry, terribly sorry that I can't say yes." Her voice broke and a sob choked her. "I wish I could say that I love you. I've tried so hard, but I can't. I just can't. I've even prayed about it, that if it was God's will, that I would fall in love with you, for I know what a wonderful work we could do together, but that prayer hasn't been answered. I don't know what's the matter with me. I've never really been in love with anyone. Perhaps I never shall be. How I wish it could be you!"

She laid a hand upon his as it rested upon the wheel and looked into his eyes while her tears hung upon her lashes. She saw the disappointment in his eyes, but he smiled and took her hand.

"Don't cry, my darling," he said in tones of tenderness. "It hurts deeply, for I was hoping so while I prayed, but I know that His will is best. Perhaps He has some better thing for both of us, though I fail to see how that could be. I shall carry a lonely heart to the field with me, but perhaps it is that loneliness and heartache that will make it easier for me to understand the suffering of those who do not have the hope that I have."

"Oh, Mark, you are so wonderful!" she exclaimed. "It would be such an honor to be your wife and to share your work with you. How I wish that it could be!"

"Let's not let this make any difference in our relationship in our work," he said. "Just pretend that I have never said a word. Let us continue to be friends and fellow workers for the Lord. Will you?"

"Of course, Mark, dear," she said and smiled through her tears. "It has been such a joy to work with you. I shall always look back upon these months as the happiest ones of my life. And I know that the Lord will bring greater happiness to you than I ever could."

He smiled a rather crooked smile as he said, "That's hard to believe, but I know that God is able."

"That's my motto also," she said as she told him good-by and went inside. Tears were coursing down her cheeks as she went to her room.

CHAPTER **13**

IT HAD BEEN RAINING FOR DAYS and this afternoon the rain still kept persistently falling, pouring a steady stream from low-hanging clouds on the already drenched land.

In spite of the rain Meredith went out to see Mrs. Field. She had not been there for several days and she knew how lonely the old lady was there in the little house all alone.

Mrs. Field's strength was fading perceptibly and Meredith knew that her days were really numbered. She looked forward happily to her homegoing. Meredith listened to her talk as if she were going on an earthly journey to some home of the long ago and her heart was too full for words. She would miss this dear friend, for she had learned to look forward to her visits and she loved the old lady dearly. She felt as if she had known her all her life for she was much like Granny.

She took with her a box of candy which Terry had given her and some of the flowers he had insisted upon sending. They sat talking while the old lady nibbled on the candy.

"It's a pity to waste that young man's gifts on me," she remarked, "but I do enjoy them just the same as if they were meant for me. It's sweet of you to share them with me."

"If I ate all that candy, I'd be so fat that he wouldn't want to bring me any more and then we'd both feel neglected," Meredith said with a laugh.

They sat near the window while they talked and Meredith looked out upon the rain-soaked road and wondered when the skies would be clear again. Those tires of hers were getting pretty worn and the car skidded dangerously every time she turned a curve or put on the brakes. She really should get a new car. This old jalopy should be put aside, for it had served its purpose long ago. She disliked the thought of spending money for a new car when there were so many better places she could think of where that money was needed.

Presently a truck approached and she saw that it was the prison truck. As it drew nearer there was a loud report and the truck began to lurch crazily, then skidded across the road and landed on its side on the soft shoulder of the road.

"What happened?" Mrs. Field asked as Meredith rushed to the door and looked out.

"It's the prison truck and it blew a tire," Meredith cried. "Bill is out there and he may be hurt. He's under the truck."

She did not wait for raincoat or galoshes but ran out into the rain to the truck. Just as she got there she saw Bill struggling to get out from under the seat.

"Oh, Bill! Are you hurt? Can I help you?" she cried in distress as she saw his face contract with pain.

"I've got a sprained ankle or else it's broken," he said as he managed to extricate himself.

He leaned against the side of the truck and felt of his ankle.

"I don't think it's broken," he said, "only sprained. If you'll phone the prison and tell them what happened, I'd appreciate it. And you'd better get in out of this rain or you'll catch cold."

"How about you?" she asked. "You're not going to stay out here and wait for help to come. You'll catch cold yourself."

"It doesn't matter about me," he said with the old note of bitterness in his voice.

"I'm not leaving you here. Come on in the house and wait there until help comes. I'll help you. Just lean on me."

Though he winced with pain, he managed with her help to hobble to the house. Mrs. Field was at the door waiting for them.

"Come in," she invited. "It's chilly out here. I'll light a fire in the kitchen and you can dry those wet clothes."

"I'd best wait out here," Bill said. "I don't think I should go in."

"Nonsense," Meredith said as she urged him through the door. "We both need to dry as fast as possible and that ankle needs attention. Perhaps we can find some wide adhesive tape. That will help after we soak that ankle in hot water for a while."

"I must phone the prison and let them know what happened," Bill said as she helped him into the kitchen.

"We'll phone later," Meredith said. "Right now we'll attend to you."

She drew hot water in a small tub that Mrs. Field had brought.

"I forgot to introduce you," Meredith said while Bill removed his shoe. "This is Bill, Mrs. Field, Bill Gordon. He's the man who helped me with my car that first day I came to Cedarville. He works at the prison."

Mrs. Field gave Bill a smile and said that she hoped his ankle was not too badly sprained, then she went to look for the adhesive. She brought it in and then left them, saying that if they needed her, she would be in the next room.

"Why didn't you tell her the truth, that I'm a criminal, a murderer and a robber?" he asked when Mrs. Field had left.

She met his clouded eyes with her warm friendly gaze.

"Because there was no need to tell her," she told him. "It wouldn't have made any difference to her. You are someone in trouble and she is a wonderful Christian. She would feel as I do about you."

"And how is that?" he asked in cynical tones.

"The same as I always have," she replied as she met his eyes that were now questioning and just a little anxious. "You are someone for whom Christ died and you need the comfort and peace which only He can give."

"Then you don't think that I'm not much better than a savage beast?"

"Of course not."

"But I saw the shock and horror in your eyes when that rat told you about me."

"I was shocked," she admitted, "for I didn't dream that you were a prisoner. I don't know why I didn't guess you were when I knew that you were driving the prison truck, but I just thought that you were someone who hadn't had a fair chance in life and that was why you were so bitter."

"I haven't had a fair chance," he said harshly. "If there is a God in heaven, He knows that I haven't. Why shouldn't I be bitter? When Stuart told you about me, he didn't dare tell you the truth about himself." His eyes blazed with the bright look of hate. "He said that I was little better than a savage beast. Well, I think he's lower than a beast. A beast kills in order to survive or to get food. He kills for the money it gives him."

"What do you mean by that?" she asked in shocked surprise.

"He's the official executioner. He gets a bonus for every man who is sent to the chair. He gets paid well for pulling that switch that sends a man to his death."

"Oh!" she cried in a shocked whisper while she stared wide-eyed at him. "Is that why you hate him so?" she asked presently.

"No. I despise him for that, but that's not why I hate him. He was on the jury that condemned me to life imprisonment, with no chance for a parole or pardon. When I warned the warden a short while ago and helped to stop a riot in the prison, Stuart did everything in his power to prevent them from rewarding me by making me a trusty. It was contrary to regulations and that self-righteous hypocrite called the rules on the warden. But the warden got permission to set aside the rules because of what I had done. Stuart would be only too glad for an excuse to have that privilege taken from me. If it hadn't been for you that day, he would have done it."

"I could never let that happen," she told him, "because I would have been the cause of it."

She emptied the water which had cooled and put more hot water in the tub.

"Hasn't that helped a lot?" she asked. "I know, because I sprained my ankle once and I know how it helped me."

He told her that it did and a silence fell between them.

"I'd better get word to the prison," he remarked presently. "They'll be expecting me, for I'm late already. They'll be out searching for me if I don't let them know and I'll be in trouble. There's always the possibility of a trusty breaking his trust and trying to make a getaway. That always makes me worry when I'm late."

"And I've made you late more than once," she said regretfully. "I'm sorry. I'll phone just as soon as I get that ankle bandaged and I promise that you won't be in any trouble this time because you're late."

Their eyes met in a sudden silence and there crept into his a look which swept away all the hardness. It was a look of pleading which touched her strangely.

"I suppose it wouldn't do any good for me to tell you that I'm no killer and no robber, that I'm not guilty of the crime for which I am serving sentence."

The doubt and the questioning which had disturbed her so constantly and the conviction which she had reluctantly been forced to accept, were all wiped out by his words and the look in his eyes. She felt instinctively that he was telling her the truth.

"I believe you," she said. "I didn't believe Terry at first, but when he gave me the details later on, I was forced to believe that perhaps you were guilty. But now I do believe that you are innocent."

He smiled crookedly. "Then you're the only one who does believe I'm innocent. The jury pronounced me guilty and everyone else there at that trial thought I was. If there hadn't been a doubt in the minds of some of the experts who examined that body, I would have been electrocuted long ago and your friend Terry would have received his bonus for my death."

"Forgive me," he said as he saw her wince. "I do thank you for believing in me. You'll never know how much it means to me to have you believe in me. That will be one small comfort to carry with me through the years."

"If Terry Stuart is what you say he is, how could he have served on the jury? That surely is a most unusual procedure."

"He didn't get the job here at the prison until after I was sentenced. The warden's deputy had to leave a few months after I entered prison and Terry got the job."

Mrs. Field came in just then and asked how the ankle was getting along. She stood by while Meredith bandaged the injured ankle. She made a boot with strips of tape, leaving a small opening at the front to allow room for swelling.

"I'll never be able to repay both of you for your kindness," he said when she had finished. "You're as good as a doctor," he said with a smile at Meredith. "It feels so much better that I think I can walk on it. How did you learn to bandage like that?"

"Experience and directions from an old book of medicine taught me," she told him. "It helped me so much with my own sprained ankle that I decided to use it in the future with all my patients." She gave him a smile. "Now I'll phone and get help for you and the truck."

When the wrecker finally arrived and Bill had gone, Mrs. Field turned to her with eyes of sympathy.

"How I pity that poor young man," she said. "He doesn't look like a criminal. Somehow I don't believe that he should be there in that prison."

"I was sure that you heard what we said," Meredith replied. "You couldn't help it and I'm glad that you did."

"Yes, I was waiting in the next room and I couldn't help but hear for the door was open. I knew you wouldn't mind. My heart goes out to that young man. He's so far from God and he needs the comfort that God can give."

"My heart went out to him for that same reason the first time I met him," Meredith told her. "He is so bitter and so hopeless and defeated. I'm glad that I know the truth now."

"Do you believe what he told you?" Mrs. Field asked.

"Yes, I do. I don't understand just how it all happened, but I can't help but believe that some terrible mistake has been made. I shall pray that God will bring about his release if he is innocent. And I believe that he is.''

"I shall join you, my dear," Mrs. Field said. "We shall both pray for his release and his salvation."

"Either one will take a miracle," Meredith said with a sigh.

"He is quite a good-looking young man, even in his soaked muddy clothes," the old lady remarked while her keen gaze rested upon Meredith's face.

Meredith felt herself coloring under the other's scrutiny and blurted out in embarrassment, "No matter what he looks like, he is precious in God's sight and I wish above everything that his soul may be saved. As we have said, it will take a miracle. But," she added with a smile, "He is able, I know He's able."

Mrs. Field bent over and kissed Meredith's flushed cheek.

"I'm sure He is," she whispered. "And I know that prayer can work miracles."

CHAPTER 14

MEREDITH HAD NO WAY OF KNOWING how Bill's injured ankle had progressed. On her visits to Mrs. Field she saw no sign of the prison truck. She wondered whether Bill had been punished for the accident or whether he was able to drive the truck. She continued to pray that in some way the Lord would perform a miracle and not only save his soul, but that his innocence might be proved. This last seemed almost more impossible than the first, but she had faith to believe in the impossible.

Mrs. Field brought the subject up once when there had been another rain.

"I wonder how that young man is getting along. I've watched for the truck to pass here but I haven't seen him. I do hope that his ankle is well by now."

"So do I," Meredith said, "but there is no way we can find out. Perhaps the truck was damaged so badly that it has taken a long time to repair it."

"I still pray for that boy," the old lady said. "In spite of those hard cynical words and his unbelief, I somehow feel that God will bring him around and he will have a new start in life."

"I hope so, but sometimes my faith is rather weak," Meredith said.

She found out later why they had not seen the truck. This information came through a man at the garage. She overheard him asking someone when the new trucks for the prison would arrive.

"It's about time they got new ones," he commented.

"No wonder that old hunk of junk blew a tire. It was long past going."

Meredith could not refrain from asking about Bill.

"Do you know what happened to the man who was driving that truck when it turned over? It happened in front of my friend's house. We took him in out of the rain. He had a badly sprained ankle and I wonder how he got along."

"I wouldn't know about that," the man told her.

Meredith thought that he looked at her rather curiously. She wondered if he remembered she had been there before to report about the truck.

When she went to the prison with Mark for their service, she hoped that she might find out something or catch a glimpse of Bill. She wished that he would come to the service but he did not come.

One afternoon as she was coming out of a store, she met him going in. The new truck was outside. He gave her a smile and was about to pass her without speaking. She knew the reason why, now, but she was determined not to let him go without a word.

"I'm glad your ankle is well again," she remarked when she noticed that he was not limping.

"Yes, thanks to your good treatment," he told her. "The doctor didn't do a thing when he saw what a good job you had done."

"I'm glad that I was able to help you when I have caused you so much trouble."

Just then the manager of the store came outside and looked at them in surprise. Meredith was quick to realize that this incident might cause more trouble for Bill and she hastened to explain.

"I was asking him about his sprained ankle," she said. "When the truck he was driving blew a tire and turned over right in front of my friend's house, he had a badly sprained ankle. We took him in out of the rain until help arrived. I'm so glad to know that he is able to be out again. He could have been killed."

The proprietor smiled understandingly while Bill left them and went inside.

103

"Do you know who that fellow is?" the proprietor asked.

"Yes, Mr. Jenkins, I know that he is a trusty."

"He's a dangerous criminal and you'd better keep away from him. I don't see why they ever let him drive that truck. One of these days he'll escape and kill someone else."

"He doesn't look like a dangerous person to me," Meredith said defensively.

Jenkins smiled. "Just like you women. Never see anything wrong with a good-looking man until it's too late and then it does no good for them to be sorry they wasted their sympathy on him."

"His looks have nothing to do with my sympathy for him," Meredith flashed indignantly. "He's a human being even if he is a prisoner. And he was hurt. Am I so foolish because I was glad to know that he was well again? I'd have that much sympathy for a wounded dog."

"I'm sorry, Miss Meredith," Jenkins said apologetically. "I didn't mean to offend. Just remember to be careful not to let your sympathy get the best of you. That fellow's not worth it."

"You just remember that a little human kindness and sympathy will never hurt anyone. It wouldn't hurt you to have a little for that terrible criminal in your store," was her parting shot.

Poor Bill, she soliloquized. The world seemed to be against him. Everyone seemed to share Terry's opinion of him. Well, she didn't, and, no matter what the world might think of him, still he had a soul for which Christ died and he needed someone who believed in him, someone who would stand by him when all the world was against him. She would pray for him while everyone despised him.

The memory of his smile and his friendly words spread a warm glow within her. It helped wipe out the anger toward Jenkins. She was glad that Terry could not ask for a date with her just now. He was studying for his law examinations and he had no time for anything else. It gave her a respite and time to think over what she should do about him. After what Bill had revealed, she had such an aversion to him that she was sure she could not hide it. She wanted nothing more to do with him, but she couldn't just dismiss him without a word of explanation and she couldn't pretend to go along as they had been doing. She was too honest to pretend something she did not feel.

Christmas drew near and the stores were crowded with weary shoppers with long lists and dwindling cash. Children began to be on their best behavior for fear that Santa would not visit them. Anxious mothers were searching for secure hiding places for packages which the prying eyes of children might discover.

It was a time when Meredith fought against the ache in her heart which seemed keener at this season. It brought back tender, yet heartbreaking memories of Granny and their quiet, yet joyous Christmases together. Granny had never deceived her about Santa Claus, but each year of her childhood that well-filled stocking met her eager eyes as she opened them at the peep of dawn. There were packages at the foot of the stocking, always the things she had most wished for. Granny had told her that she should thank the Lord for providing her with these gifts on His birthday when many forgot to give Him what He wanted most of all from them, their hearts that He might cleanse them from sin, and their love for Him which would bring peace into their lives and a joy that no Christmas gift from earthly loved ones could ever bring.

Even before she had given her life to the Lord, she had knelt with Granny beside her bed and thanked Him for all His goodness and the wonderful gifts which He had provided for her on His birthday. Their day would be quietly happy because of this and in the afternoon when friends would come in to visit them, they would share in the joy that these two experienced, for they also had the peace of God in their hearts.

Meredith contrasted those happy days with what she knew Christmas day would be with her aunt. The house would be lavishly decorated with holly and mistletoe and there would be eggnog and punch for all the visitors who dropped in, with "just a little stick in it" to make everyone feel happy — so her aunt explained.

Rev. Hawthorne would drop in during the evening to partake of the bountiful refreshments including a liberal serving of eggnog and to receive the generous check which the Bartons always gave him at this time. There would be laughter made more high-pitched and chatter from voices that became increasingly louder as the liquor began to spread its potent influence among them. And she would be the one kill-joy of the evening, unable to respond to the silly jokes and senseless chatter and refusing to drink the punch which had liquor in it.

She wished she could go away somewhere and be alone until the day was over, but she tried not to reveal her heartache and loneliness because of Granny's absence and her concern for the souls of her aunt and uncle whom she loved.

The day dawned with a glorious golden sun and a light snow which covered the landscape with its glistening whiteness. The trees stood in their shrouds of sparkling gems, lifting their transformed branches valiantly toward the God who had brought them into existence by His word and who had mantled their bareness with His feathery snowflakes. The drab winter world had changed overnight into a fairyland of silent whiteness as yet untouched by man's incessant tramping or the snow plow's inevitable approach, destroying the beauty of the perfect picture.

The household was astir early, for there was much to be done. The guests would begin to arrive in the early afternoon and throughout the evening until late into the night. The gifts were piled under the tree in the living room and after breakfast Meredith and her aunt and uncle, the maid and the cook, as well as the gardener, went into the living room to open their gifts.

Meredith was both pleased and touched as she opened the boxes containing her gifts, for each gift was just the thing she needed, yet which she had hesitated to buy for herself. It had always seemed that when she planned to buy a dress or something else for herself, she found someone who needed that money more than she did. There were two lovely dresses and a coat from her uncle and aunt.

"How wonderful you are to give me these lovely things," she said as she kissed them both and gave them a hug. "But you shouldn't have done it. You've spent too much on me and I don't deserve any of it."

"All of our love goes with them," Mrs. Barton said. "It makes us glad to be able to give them. Since you won't buy them for yourself, we're glad to get them for you."

Meredith smiled and gave her another hug.

When all the packages had been opened with many oh's and ah's from everyone, the room was put in order and Mrs. Barton busied herself with preparations for the guests while Meredith helped as much as she could. Susan, the maid, was so efficient that there was not much for either of them to do.

Terry asked if he might come around in the evening and she could not well refuse. She and Mark had planned a service at the prison for the early afternoon and they went as soon as dinner was over. As a special concession, Mark had been invited to dinner. Meredith knew how lonely he was and she wanted to have him share this day with her, for both of them knew what the day meant, not only to them, but to the whole unheeding world, little aware or caring little that the very freedom of their existence had come because of the One whose birthday they so thoughtlessly celebrated.

They drove by and picked up some of the young people who were to go with them. They carried baskets of fruit and cake and candy which Meredith had provided, and which were to be distributed among the prisoners who attended the service.

She had packed a small basket and covered it with cellophane and tied a big red bow on top. She set it carefully in the car with the admonition to the youngsters to keep it from being upset.

"Who is this for?" one of them asked.

"A man who once helped me in trouble on the highway," she explained, feeling self-conscious while she did so. "This is the only way I could think of to repay him for his kindness."

They did not ask any more questions and she was glad, but Mark looked at her with wide-eyed surprise.

"I'll tell you about him," she said in low tones.

He made no comment and she was glad for that also.

She hoped that Bill would be there for the service but he was not. After the service, when all the gifts had been distributed, she took the basket to one of the guards.

"Would you please see that Bill Gordon gets this?" she asked.

"Yes, Miss, of course," the guard replied as he took the basket.

He stared at her with interest and his eyes betrayed his curiosity.

"This is from an old lady who took him in out of the rain when his truck turned over in front of her house. I put my name on the card also, for I was there that day and helped him with his sprained ankle. I thought he would like to know that Mrs. Field remembered him."

This was true as far as it went, for Meredith had told Mrs. Field what she planned to do and asked her if she might use her name.

"Of course," the old lady told her. "I was wishing that I could do something to cheer that young man at this season and I'm glad you thought of doing this."

Meredith dreaded Terry's visit. She would try to be cordial but it would be hard for her to pretend something she did not feel and there was no cordiality in her feeling toward him, only aversion.

He came a short while after her return from the prison. The memory of those sin-marked faces with the hopeless look in some of those eyes, was still with her. Christmas meant nothing to them. Some who were in for life had nothing for the future but endless Christmas days behind prison walls. None of them knew what the day signified. It was just another endless day in a life which held no hope.

Bill was one of these, only his condition was worse, if what he had told her was true. He was here unjustly, living out his life for a crime which he did not commit. She remembered Terry's version of Bill's crime and a faint doubt assailed her. If she could only be sure that Bill had told her the truth!

What she was thinking must have been reflected in her greeting when she met Terry at the door.

"I don't seem to be very welcome," he remarked. "Were you expecting someone else?"

"Of course not. I was expecting you. I'm sorry if I didn't seem hospitable."

"Merry Christmas," he said, his good humor restored.

"Thank you and the same to you," she replied as she led the way to the library just behind the living room.

"It's been so long since I've seen you," he said as he sat down beside her. "It seems like ages to me."

"How did the exams come out?" she asked, ignoring his remark. "I'm sure you made good grades."

"I wish I could say that I did, but to be truthful, I barely made it. I shall have to buckle down to work on this second term if I ever expect to pass the bar. I've been working hard on another project," and he gave her a significant glance.

"You'd better forget that project and attend to your studies," she advised. "That other project is a waste of time."

"You're not very encouraging," he said as the smile died from his eyes. "I don't consider it a waste of time. To me it was more important than even my law course. If I hadn't worked on that project, some other fellow might have stolen you from me and then there would be no incentive to even become a lawyer."

He reached in his pocket and drew out a little box.

"I hope you'll like this," he said as he gave it to her. "I searched for a long time to find one like the one that was ruined the night you saved Cora's life."

The box contained a watch and it was lovely, even more beautiful than the one she had worn that night and had ruined in the struggle with Cora.

"I remembered that you regretted having that other one ruined and I tried to find one just like it, but this was as near as I could come to it."

She looked at it silently for a while.

"Don't you like it?" he asked in disappointment as she continued looking at it without even thanking him for it.

"Of course I do," she told him, "and I thank you for bringing it to me, but I can't wear it, Terry. I can't accept it."

He stared at her in hurt surprise.

"Why not? Why can't you wear it?"

She hesitated before she replied. Should she tell him the reason? She would have to. It would hurt and possibly make him angry, but he might as well know the truth now as later. Perhaps it was best that he should know now.

"I can't wear it, Terry, because every time I looked at it, I would feel that I was wearing something that was bought with blood money."

"What do you mean by that?" he asked, amazed and angry.

"I believe you know what I mean. I would feel that every dollar that was spent for this little watch had cost a man his life, that the money which you spent was made by sending a man out into eternity."

He looked at her aghast and was silent for a long time as she faced his stare with eyes that did not waver, but which were filled with a great sadness. Slowly it dawned upon him that she knew the truth. His face went white.

"How did you know?" he asked slowly.

"Does it matter? Oh, Terry, how could you! How could you!"

"Why is that so terrible?" he demanded defensively as he regained his composure. "Someone had to do it. I did it to help my uncle when the other man left and there was no one else qualified as an electrician to do the job."

"You did it for the money also, didn't you?" she asked quietly.

Her eyes spoke volumes which she did not utter.

"What if I did?" he retorted. "Those men have to die and I needed that extra money. The law demands that they should be executed. I'm only doing what the law requires. Am I any worse than a soldier who gets paid to kill?"

"Yes, I think you are," she said. "The soldier kills because he's protecting his country and not for the money. He kills an enemy who would destroy his country."

"What do you call a condemned criminal but an enemy

of society who would destroy it if he were allowed to go free?'' he demanded.

"I'm not able to argue with you on that, Terry, and it will do no good for me to try, but to me, what you are doing is horrible. Perhaps I am wrong, but that is the way I feel about it.''

"Don't you believe in capital punishment?'' he asked.

"Yes, I do. It was God's law from the time of Noah and He has never changed it, but I don't see how anyone could take money for sending a man out into eternity.''

"What would you do to carry out God's law?'' he asked with bitter sarcasm.

"I don't know, perhaps I'd do what they do when a man faces a firing squad. I'd have some of them with real bullets and some with empty cartridges, then no one would know who had fired the fatal shots. It seems to me that what you are doing tends to make a man ruthless, with little regard for human life or immortal souls.''

She put the watch back in the box and handed it to him.

"I'm sorry I can't wear it, Terry. Please believe that I am. But I just can't.''

"You found out about that from Bill Gordon,'' he said as his anger mounted. "He must have told you the day that truck was wrecked. He broke the rules again when he told you that. That is always kept a secret, even from the prisoners. Sometimes they manage to find it out.''

She was silent. She realized that Terry was bound to know about the wreck and that Bill had been taken in while he waited for help. Of course Terry could put two and two together, for there was no other way for her to have discovered the truth.

"If this is the way you feel about me, I'd better not stay,'' he said as he put the box back in his pocket.

"That's up to you,'' she said.

He rose abruptly and she followed him to the door. Her eyes were troubled as she saw him go, for she heard him say under his breath as he started down the steps, "I'll get him for this!''

She went to her room and remained there until her aunt

called her to come down and join her with their guests who had just come in. She was down in the depths again. There would be more trouble for Bill and she would have been the cause of it. What hurt still more, was the fact that she could do nothing to prevent it. It seemed that she had done nothing but bring trouble upon him. And she so much wanted to help him!

She was glad when the last guest had departed and she could go back to her room where she could be alone with her thoughts. But those thoughts robbed her of sleep for long hours.

CHAPTER 15

TERRY LEFT MEREDITH AND GOT into his car while rage seethed within him, a mad swirl of fury that would have led him to kill if the object of his wrath had been near at hand. He blamed Bill Gordon for what he had brought upon himself. He forgot his own foolish display of hatred against Bill and his desire for revenge that had brought the first rift between him and the girl he loved.

His one desire now, as he drove recklessly through the night, was to make Bill suffer for something for which Bill was not to blame. Like all self-righteous, spiteful, egotistical natures, he would not admit his own guilt, but sought to place the blame on someone else.

He had hated Bill even before Bill had made him ridiculous when Bill had been the means of heading off the riot in prison. From the time of the trial when he had been on the jury which had pronounced Bill guilty, that hatred had grown until now it had reached its climax and he was determined to make Bill suffer.

He knew when he first took up his duties at the prison, that Bill recognized him and hated him because of that. Bill had not tried to hide that hatred or his contempt for him when the secret leaked out that Terry was the official executioner. He had displayed that contempt in a way that made Terry furious because he could not do anything about it. It was displayed in every look from Bill's eyes whenever they met and by his manner even when he obeyed orders.

Bill had been a model prisoner and had won the warden's friendship and Terry dared not protest his uncle's interest in the prisoner. It irked Terry because there was nothing he could find against Bill even though he tried to, so that he could put Bill under prison discipline.

When Bill was made a trusty, Terry was furious, but he knew better than to reveal his feelings toward Bill to his uncle. Mr. Harris, the warden, was not in the least like his nephew. He was kind as well as just and, though he adhered strictly to prison rules, he had a sympathy for prisoners who seemed to be trying to atone for their crimes by their good behavior.

Now this had to happen to top it all. He felt that he could never regain his relationship with Meredith and that was the hardest blow he had ever received, for he loved her with all the love of his selfish, egotistical heart. He had never had a doubt until now, that one day she would succumb to his persistence and give him her love. He had never failed before and he had set out many times to win a girl's love, just for the satisfaction it gave him to know that he could. Now, what he wanted more than anything else seemed lost to him and he fumed in impotent rage as he realized this. And Bill was to blame, he told himself, as he tried to think of some way to make him suffer and of some way by which he could win Meredith's friendship again.

The next morning he was at the prison early, hoping that his uncle had not yet come into his office. He was disappointed to find him there inspecting some reports.

"I'd like to have Bill Gordon brought in," he said. "There's something I want to question him about."

"About what?" asked Mr. Harris. Terry's wrathful look made him suspicious.

"About a rule that he has broken," Terry said, trying not to let his anger be revealed.

Mr. Harris gave an order and Bill was brought in. He had no valid reason for refusing his nephew's request.

When Bill was brought in Terry faced him furiously and angry words burst from him.

"How dare you break prison rules and let an outsider know that I am the official executioner?" he blazed.

"That's no secret," Bill retorted. Everyone in here knows it and they despise you for it."

Terry raised his hand to strike Bill, but Mr. Harris put out an intervening hand and stopped him.

"Watch yourself, Terry," he warned. "No rough stuff in here."

"You told that girl and turned her against me!" Terry cried in uncontrolled fury.

Bill's eyes flashed. "Don't speak of her as 'that girl'. She's a lady and she deserves your respect when you speak of her."

"Why did you tell her what I was?" Terry demanded.

"Because you told her what I was," Bill retorted. "You told her that I was little better than a savage beast, so why shouldn't I tell her that you were not as good as that? You tried to make her despise me, so why shouldn't I tell her the truth about you before she should make the mistake of falling in love with you?"

Terry's eyes flashed fire and his fists clenched as he struggled against the desire to strike Bill. He gazed at Bill while an evil smile twisted his lips.

"What difference should it make to you what she thinks of you? Perhaps you've had the nerve to fall in love with her yourself. She wouldn't wipe her foot on you. Because you can never hope to have her think of you with anything but contempt, you've tried to turn her against me."

Bill's hand shot out and landed a blow upon Terry's chin that sent him sprawling. Mr. Harris rose and approached him while Terry picked himself up from the floor.

"I'm sorry, Bill," Mr. Harris said, "but you know what this means. You've struck a prison official. I shall have to enforce the rules and see that you pay the penalty."

"Yes!" Terry cried as he felt his chin while his eyes blazed their fury. "He deserves to be put into solitary. I demand that he be put there and left for the full limit."

"You should be put there yourself," Mr. Harris said sternly. "You deliberately baited him to striking you. You deserved what you got!"

"I'm sorry I did it, warden," Bill said apologetically.

"That won't get you anywhere," Terry stormed. "You'll pay for both your crimes."

"Be quiet, Terry," Mr. Harris commanded. "He hasn't committed any crime. He'll be sufficiently punished for what he has done, so that ought to satisfy you, even though I hate to do it."

He called for a guard and Bill was led away to solitary confinement which was calculated to bring the most recalcitrant prisoner to obedience.

Terry was appeased for the time being, for he knew what solitary meant and he was determined to see that Bill remained there as long as possible. His hate and desire for revenge had been appeased but not wiped out.

His problem about Meredith worried him more as time passed. He was ashamed of himself for the way he had brought Meredith into his argument with Bill, but he justified himself by the results, even though he had had the humiliation of being knocked down because of it. One day Bill would pay for this, if it was in his power to make that possible. But he did not know what to do to restore himself to Meredith's favor.

His pride urged him to forget her but he could not. As the days passed, the only glimpse he caught of her was her lovely profile as she sat in the pew across from him in church. When the service was ended and he tried to catch her eye, so that he could give her a smile and a pleading look, she went out without ever turning her eyes in his direction, although he knew that she knew he was there waiting to speak to her. He spent hours during sleepless nights trying to plan some way of approach, but he could think of nothing.

One thought came to him as the only means of getting back into her good graces. That was that he should tell her that he would give up his position as prison executioner. He was not willing to do that, for he needed the money. Besides, he argued, why should he do that when there were so few executions during the year? She would never know the truth unless Bill should tell her and he was sure that this would never happen.

While he was worrying over his problem, Meredith was

wondering if anything had happened to Bill. She felt sure that Terry would hate Bill more than ever and that he would try in some way to make Bill suffer. She regretted that she had told Terry what Bill had told her. At the moment she did not realize that this might bring more trouble to Bill. She could have returned the watch without telling him the real reason why she could not wear it. But any other reason would not have been the truth and she couldn't go on with him and pretend that she felt the same toward him.

One day she saw the truck stop in front of the store and a strange driver was at the wheel. Then she was sure that something had happened to Bill. What could Terry have done, she wondered. She thought of calling Terry and letting him come to see her so that she could ask him about Bill, but she knew that this would do no good. He would likely not tell her the truth and it might even make him more angry with Bill. She tried to forget the whole miserable affair but she could not.

Mark saw how unhappy she was but he wisely kept silent. He felt that if she wanted to talk to him and tell him what was worrying her, she would, and that if she didn't, she might feel that he was prying.

On a Sunday afternoon when the service was over and she and Mark, followed by the youngsters were passing down one of the corridors past a row of cells, she caught her breath sharply, for she saw Bill standing there behind the bars. He was looking at her while his hands clenched the bars tightly. When she stopped and spoke his name in a surprised whisper, he turned his back upon her without replying. She stood there a moment, longing to say something, while Mark and the others stood at one side, surprised and curious. Then the guard told them to move on.

"It's against the rules, Miss," he said, "to speak to any of the prisoners except on visiting days or by special permission from the warden."

When they had taken the youngsters home and she and Mark were alone, she told Mark all about Bill.

"That's what has been worrying you lately," he said when she had finished.

"Yes. I feel that I have brought nothing but trouble to him when I was so anxious to help him. I feel sure that he must hate me. I wish I could do something to undo all the harm I have done."

He put his hand over hers and gave her a look which he seldom allowed her to see.

"No one could ever hate you, Meredith," he said gently. "I'm sure he doesn't."

His words and the look that went with them did not add to her peace of mind. How she wished that Mark would stop loving her or that she could fall in love with him! He meant more to her than anyone else she knew and yet she was hurting him and would have to hurt him more if he had to go to the field alone.

"If I could only talk to him and make him understand how much I'd like to help him and how sorry I am that I've only hurt him."

"Why not go to see him on visiting day," he suggested. "You would have a chance to talk to him then. I'm sure you can make him understand."

"Why didn't I think of that?" and she gave him a bright smile. "What would I do without you?"

What shall I ever do without you? Mark thought sadly as he returned her smile.

CHAPTER 16

MEREDITH WAITED NERVOUSLY FOR BILL to be brought into the visitors' room. She had caught the guard's commiserating glance as she gave his name and she colored under it.

Bill came in and greeted her with a nod in response to her smile then sat silently waiting for her to speak. His sombre look did not give her much encouragement to begin. Bill had come only under pressure. When the guard told him that he had a visitor he said that he didn't want to see anyone and that he wouldn't go to see them.

"I can't imagine anyone wanting to see me and I don't want to see anyone," he said.

"There's a young lady waiting in there to see you and I'm not going to let her leave without seeing you," the guard told him. He unlocked the door and said, "Get going," as Bill hesitated.

Meredith saw how pale and emaciated Bill looked and she asked with concern in her voice, "Have you been sick?"

"Being in solitary doesn't help to make one healthy," he replied as his eyes met hers for a moment, then were lowered again.

She found it hard to talk to him when others were talking all about her on the same side of the screen which separated the visitors from the prisoners and with the guard standing not far away, but her concern for Bill helped her to forget everything else.

"Oh!" she breathed. Her exclamation and the tone of her voice expressed her shock.

She knew only too well what solitary meant, darkness

and dampness with only bread and water. "Why did they put you there?" she asked anxiously.

He looked at her with a sudden spark in his eyes.

"You should ask your boy friend that," he said harshly. "I hit him. That was a criminal offense and they put me there. Worst of all, they took away my liberty. Now I'll spend the rest of my life behind these bars."

"Oh, Bill! I'm so sorry!" she said. "You're wrong about Terry. He isn't my boy friend, just a friend. Since I found out what he is, I don't even want him for a friend. What did he do to make you hit him when you knew what the consequences would be?"

"He said something I couldn't let pass. He was furious because I had told you the truth about him. I never thought you'd tell him."

There was accusation in his eyes and it hurt her, for she felt guilty.

"I'm sorry I told him that I knew. I didn't tell him that you told me, but of course he guessed that it was you. I felt that I had to tell him, but I never would have if I had thought that this would have happened to you. You see, he gave me a watch for Christmas and I told him that I couldn't accept it. I told him why I couldn't. I felt that it was bought with blood money that he had received for taking the lives of men, even though they were condemned to die. Perhaps it was foolish for me to feel that way, but I did and I had to be honest with him."

"No wonder he was so furious with me," Bill remarked. His voice had lost its harshness and his eyes were no longer hostile.

"Please believe how sorry I am," she begged. "I'm going to try to help you get your liberty back."

"Please don't. You'll only make it worse for me."

"I don't blame you for feeling that way, but I want to try anyway," she argued. "But before I do, I shall pray about it, for I don't want to make any more mistakes and get you into further trouble."

He did not reply but she saw the cynical smile flit across his lips.

"I know that you don't believe in prayer, but I do," she said.

She saw that it was almost time for her to go and she turned to him with appeal in her eyes and deep concern in her voice.

"Let me say this before I go. I don't know why I have been so concerned about you from the very first time I met you, but I know that there is a reason for it. I know that God has a purpose for everything that He allows to happen to a Christian and I know that He had a reason for everything that has happened between us. Mrs. Field and I are both praying that in some way, somehow, everything will work out for good to you. And I know that God is able."

He was silent while she spoke, but the cynical light gradually left his eyes and he lowered them while he bowed his head. When she had finished, he said in low tones that she scarcely heard, "I wish I had your faith. It would help now."

"I shall pray for you every day," she told him. "I feel sure that God will answer prayer."

Her time was up and the guard came to take Bill back to his cell.

"Thank you for coming," he said. "Please come again."

"I shall." She smiled tremulously as he left her.

She prayed as she walked down the cold, dim corridor which was flanked with the iron bars on both sides, prayed that one day Bill might have the peace and comfort which he needed. As she glanced at the men in the cells she passed, the great burden of their lost souls weighed heavily upon her. Why was it so easy to go down the broad highway that leads to destruction when the strait and narrow road that leads to glory is made wonderfully worth while even though it seems unattractive to those who have never taken a step toward the light that shines at the end of the road? How she wished that she could make all these sin-laden souls see what they had missed and what they could have if they would only believe.

True to her determination to try to undo the harm she had brought to Bill, she spoke to Terry the next Sunday at church.

"Would you mind coming around the first evening you have off?" she asked. "I'd like to talk to you about something."

He was pleased as well as surprised, but also just a little uneasy, but he was quick to tell her he had the next evening off and he was there promptly on time. He wondered if she knew what had happened between Bill and himself. He was prepared to do or say anything that would renew the old relationship.

"I suppose you know why I asked you to come," she told him.

"I haven't the slightest idea," he replied. "But, whatever the reason, I'm glad that you let me come again. It has hurt so terribly, Meredith, to know that you were angry with me."

"It wasn't anger, Terry. It was something that went deeper than anger. But that's not what I want to talk about now. I asked you to come so that I could talk to you about Bill Gordon."

Her words brought a quick spark of anger to his eyes.

"What is there to discuss about him? Why do you persist in being so much interested in that criminal?"

"You ought to know," she retorted. "Just because he was kind enough to help me out of trouble, he got into trouble. I feel that I am to blame and I want to do something about it."

"I think you've done that already," he said. "I told you that I would not report him to the warden and I kept my promise. What else could I do?"

"You know that that is not what I'm talking about," she said. "I'm talking about what you did to him because of what I told you Christmas night. You vented your rage against him and had him put in solitary confinement and you had his liberty taken away from him."

"He brought that on himself," Terry replied defensively. "When I reprimanded him for breaking prison rules he struck me. The warden was a witness to Bill's attack and he was the one who had Gordon put in solitary. He had to keep prison rules. You ought to know that."

"You must have said something pretty terrible to him to make him forget the consequences and strike you."

"That hot head doesn't need much provocation to make him want to fight. When a man has killed once, it is easy to harbor murder in his heart. He hates me because I represent the law and he is a criminal under sentence of the law that I'm there to uphold."

"You hate him as much as he hates you," she said accusingly. "You showed it that day when you threatened to report him."

"Did you only ask me here to tell me about my faults?" he asked. "I thought that you were going to prove that you were a Christian, the kind you claim to be, and that you were going to forgive me for my shortcomings."

She gave him a look of contempt which stung him.

"That was pretty small of you, Terry. Suppose you practice what you pretend to be and do something for Bill to undo what he has suffered because of me."

"I'll do anything possible if you'll promise to be friends again and let me come to see you."

"If you really mean that, then do what you can to persuade the warden to give Bill his liberty again. Have him restored as a trusty. It's so little when he has a lifetime of prison ahead of him with not even the hope of a parole."

Terry threw up his hands and exclaimed, "Now you are asking the impossible. That is out of my hands entirely."

"It wasn't out of your hands when you brought it all on him," she retorted. "You can at least try. And I mean try, not just pretend to try. If you don't, I shall take steps myself to see what I can do, even if it means going to the governor."

"If you do, you will only compromise yourself," he warned.

"What do I care about that?" she blazed. "I don't mind that if there is a chance of helping a man I have innocently brought trouble to. If you want me for your friend again, then do your best to undo what you have done."

"I'll do everything in my power," he promised. "Would it help you to forgive me and to forget, if I told you that I had given up my job as executioner?'' He injected a note of pleading into his voice.

Her face brightened. ''Have you? Oh, I'm so glad!'' she said as he nodded assent.

''Then may I come again soon, if I promise to do what I can about Gordon?''

''Let's wait and see what happens when you really try,'' she said.

He left her, fuming inwardly. He really did not know whether he could do anything for Bill and he was sure that he did not want to, but he wanted her friendship more than he wanted revenge upon Bill. This little visit, even though it had been so unpleasant, had made him realize how much he had suffered under her coldness. However, it made him even more furious with Bill for being the cause of it all. He wished that something would intervene to make her forget Bill and kill her interest in him.

If he could have looked into the future and could have seen just what would intervene and what his part in that future event would be, perhaps he would have forgotten Bill himself as well as his hate which would lead him on into the depths of despair.

CHAPTER 17

MRS. FIELD WAS DYING. She was in no pain, just growing weaker day by day.

"The old machinery is just about worn out," she told Meredith the day she came in and found the old lady unable to get up. "It won't be long now before your Granny and I shall meet. I shall tell her all about you."

She spoke with such assurance that Meredith believed her though she was not too sure just how much those who had gone on before would be allowed to know about what went on on earth. She knew from her Bible that they would know one another, for she had read that verse in I Corinthians, the thirteenth chapter which said that "then I shall know even as I am known." It had meant so much more to her after her grandmother had left her.

"I shall miss you so much," Meredith said, trying to repress a sob. "It's almost like saying good-by to Granny all over again."

"I know, dear," Mrs. Field said as she put out one frail hand and patted Meredith's as it rested beside her. "I know how hard the parting can be, for I've had to part with my last loved one. I hate to leave you, but I'll be so glad to be there with my husband and my children and all of those whom I have missed for so long. I've waited for this day ever since my Tom left me twenty years ago."

Meredith stroked her hair for she could not speak just then. Once more, in memory, she was sitting beside Granny's bedside and listening to almost the same words. Death, even when there was the hope of meeting again with those who were stricken by its relentless hand, was terrible. True, one day death would be destroyed by the One who had conquered death in His Resurrection, but it was the last enemy that would be destroyed. In the meantime even those who looked for eternal life in a city not made with hands, eternal in the heavens, would know the agony of parting and the pain of waiting.

Meredith remained the rest of the day with Mrs. Field after she had telephoned her aunt and told her of Mrs. Field's condition. Mrs. Barton sent the doctor, but when he came he told Meredith frankly that there was nothing medical science could do.

"Her heart is just worn out," he said. "She has known for some time that it was wearing out, but I think she was glad when I told her. She just doesn't want to live. Poor old soul! I don't much blame her. What is there for her to live for, all alone here and too old to really enjoy life?"

"That's not the reason," Meredith told him gravely. "She's just eager to go home and to be with those she loves who are waiting for her up there with the Lord."

The doctor shrugged and smiled at her as he picked up his bag.

"That's good for those who believe it," he remarked.

"Don't you believe in a life after death?" she asked in surprise.

Dr. Carver was a member of the board at the church her aunt attended.

"I have a reasonable doubt," he replied. "Men of science, especially in the medical profession, are not inclined to accept the fact that there is a soul. We can find no evidence of it in the human anatomy in experiments in surgery."

"Then you believe that man is just a higher form of animal life and that in reality we are no different from dogs or monkeys — or the missing link which science has also failed to find."

"I wouldn't put it that bluntly," he said with a smile which nettled her while it made her pity him.

"I thank God that all doctors are not such skeptics," she flashed. "The dear old doctor who brought me into the world and who is still living, not only believes that there is a soul, but he has led many of his patients to the Lord while ministering to their bodies."

"The old-fashioned family doctor," he commented with a hint of sarcasm.

"Yes, and the old-fashioned Christian who is wise enough to believe that the Bible is God's Word and to live by its teachings."

"His type is almost extinct today," the doctor remarked, nothing daunted by the rebuke in her voice and in her eyes. He felt only commiseration for her ignorance. "We live in a modern world, my dear, and must accept facts which science is constantly revealing as they are today."

"So I hear each Sunday from your pastor." She could not help it. The words he was uttering were similar to those which the Rev. Hawthorne preached, though in much more veiled and pious language.

"No matter what the modern age may be revealing," she continued, "God's word has not changed. And it is able to meet all modern scientific speculations with the truth. Either a person believes and is saved or he refuses to believe and is lost."

He patted her shoulder as he took his leave.

"If it makes you happy to believe what you do, who am I to contradict you? Let me know if there is anything I can do. I don't think it will be long. The end may come suddenly and at almost any time. It's just a question of how long her heart can go on beating."

Meredith returned to Mrs. Field with a heavy heart. Man's wisdom was foolishness compared to God's omniscience, yet man in his egotism thought himself wiser than God. He sought to prove everything by findings in the physical realm and failed to realize or believe that only spiritual truths were everlasting and that they could only be understood through the power and wisdom of the Spirit whose very existence they refused to accept.

"I could have saved you the trouble and expense of sending for the doctor," Mrs. Field told Meredith. "I knew there was nothing he could do for me. The Lord has said that my hour is almost at hand and I am just waiting for Him to say the word that will release me. Soon I shall see Him!''

"We wanted to do everything possible for you," Meredith told her as she took the frail hand in hers. "Aunt Mary is sending a nurse to be with you tonight."

"How good both of you are to me! May the Lord repay you, for He knows that I can't."

"We don't want to be repaid," Meredith assured her. "We love you and we want to do what we can for you."

She dozed for a while and Meredith sat nearby and tried to read, but she could not keep her mind on what she was trying to read. Presently the old lady opened her eyes and looked across at her.

"I won't be here to pray with you about that young man," she said, "but I'm sure that everything will work out all right for you both."

Meredith laid down the book and came over and sat beside the bed.

"Whatever made you think about him?" she asked.

"I was dreaming and he seemed to be all mixed up in that dream. I can't remember just how it was, but I do remember telling him that God's Word said, 'When thou passest through the waters I will be with thee.' Then I was singing a part of that little chorus you love to sing; 'He's able. I know He's able. He heals the brokenhearted, He sets the captive free.' '' She smiled faintly. "I never could sing. Soon I shall be able to."

"Yes," Meredith replied, with a little catch in her voice, "You'll be able to sing the song of the redeemed."

That evening when the nurse came and Meredith was driving home, she was still thinking of Mrs. Field's dream. How strange for her to be saying those words and singing that song. There was no religious significance in dreams today. There was no need of dreams when there was God's Word to be used as a guide and a warning. But she could not forget it. She wondered if Terry was really trying to get Bill put back as a trusty. She had her doubts, but time would tell. She would wait for a while and see.

Mrs. Field lingered longer than the doctor thought possible and Meredith did not get to go to the prison to see Bill for quite some time. However, there was little time to think of Bill or Terry while she sat by her friend's bedside and read to her or talked to her in the intervals when the old lady was awake. She slept for longer periods as the days passed and her strength gradually failed. One evening, as the sun was setting, feathery clouds banked the horizon. The red glow of the sun's dying glory spread a pale reflection of pink over the clouds while fingers of yellow shone through. One last, lingering ray stole into the room where Mrs. Field lay asleep and touched her face with its faint glow. Gently as a whispered answer to a call from a voice which she alone could hear, a sigh escaped her lips and a smile spread across them as her soul went out on the last gleaming ray to the land where there was no need of the sun to give its light, for the Lord of glory was the Light thereof.

Meredith saw the reflected glow on the old lady's face. It transformed her face and made it beautiful. Then the faint smile appeared and she wondered what Mrs. Field was dreaming about. She leaned over her and saw that she was not breathing. She dropped to her knees by the bed and sobbed.

The funeral ceremony was simple and there were few in attendance, for Mrs. Field had not been of enough importance for many of the church members to feel it their duty to attend the funeral. She had requested that Mark should conduct the service and Rev. Hawthorne was glad to be relieved of the duty. Mark had been to see the old lady with Meredith and she had learned to love him for what he believed and what he was doing for the Lord.

Mrs. Barton listened to the short message with disapproval at first, for she had expected her pastor to conduct the service, but as Mark spoke so sympathetically of Mrs. Field's life and her longing to go to be with the Lord and her loved ones, and as he told of what a blessing her life had been to those who knew her, she was touched and tears came to her eyes. She admitted secretly and grudgingly that her pastor would not have given a message that would have been as inspiring and as touching to the few who were there. It somehow made her wonder what it was that Mrs. Field had which she did not possess. She knew that to her, death was a horrible thing, not something to be eagerly awaited as a release from loneliness and a joyful homegoing. Was she wrong, after all, and were Meredith and Mrs. Field right? They all couldn't be right, for Meredith had as much as told her that she was not right with God. Though it had made her angry, she now began to feel that perhaps there was something wrong with her spiritual state. She tried to brush the disturbing thought aside, but it would not leave her. Could her pastor be wrong in what he preached, that by good deeds and right thinking, a person could make of himself what was expected of a Christian?

She knew that this was not what Meredith believed. But then she had argued that Meredith had gotten these old-fashioned ideas from her grandmother. Now, in the face of this friend's death, which had been such a peaceful and joyous homegoing, she knew that there was something lacking in her own spiritual experience. Someday she would have a talk with Meredith and find out just what the trouble was. She had not been willing to examine herself until now, for she had rested secure in her self-righteousness and in her pastor's words of commendation.

When the service was over and Meredith returned home with Mark, she thanked him for what he had said at the funeral.

"What you said was so true and it was so much needed for those who were there. I do hope that Aunt Mary really listened. She needed those words. I shall pray that they may bear fruit in her heart."

She went to her room and gave way once more to tears. She now felt doubly alone. Her grief over Granny was lived over again in this new grief. While her tears flowed she knelt by the bed and prayed. She knew that the only real comfort she could find was from the One who had never failed to bring peace to her heart when it was troubled or hurt.

As she fell asleep she was wondering if the two had met by now and, if they had, if they were thinking of her. One day she would know, but not now.

CHAPTER 18

WHEN MEREDITH WAS FINALLY ABLE to visit Bill again, he needed no urging from the guard to go to see her.

"I thought you had decided not to come again," he said as he took his place on the other side of the screen.

"I promised, didn't I?"

She was pleased to see that he seemed glad to see her and that there was no animosity in his attitude this time.

He admitted that she had promised, but the shrug that went with his answer told her plainly that he was not accustomed to having people keep their promises.

"I couldn't come before," she told him. "Mrs. Field was ill for quite a while before she went to be with the Lord. I was with her every day because she had no one else."

"I'm sorry that she died," he said. "I know you will miss her."

"Yes, I feel terribly lonely without her, but I can't grieve too much, because I know how happy she is now with those she loves and to be with the Lord she has served all these years."

He didn't reply, but his eyes were bleak and unbelieving.

"I wish you could have seen her go," Meredith continued. "It was so beautiful. The sun shone through the window and it spread a glow over her face and suddenly all the lines seemed to vanish and she looked young again. She went out with such a lovely smile on her lips. I really felt guilty because I cried, but I couldn't help it. I almost wished that I could have gone with her."

"I should be wishing that, not you," he said with a trace of the old bitterness in his voice. "You've got your life ahead of you. You're free to live it the way you want to. I've got nothing but these prison walls. Sometimes I feel like ending it all."

"But you're not ready to die," she told him as her eyes looked into his disconsolate ones. "How I would hate to see you go out into eternity without Christ! I wish I could make you understand just what I mean when I say what Mrs. Field often said to me. She used to say, 'I'm willing to wait God's time to call me home, but I feel as Paul did. I'm willing rather to be absent from the body and present with the Lord.'"

"I'm as ready as I'll ever be." A sigh escaped him. "I wish I had your faith, but I don't and I suppose I never will."

"You could if you want it," she said eagerly and hopefully.

She longed to penetrate that wall of indifference and unbelief and to impart to him the peace and hope which he needed, but his expression told her that just now there was no hope of doing that.

"Mrs. Field had the strangest dream not long before she died," she told him. "It was about you."

"About me? What did she dream?" he asked, interested at once.

"She said that it was so mixed up that she couldn't quite remember it, but she remembered quoting a verse from the Bible to you. Would you like to hear it?"

"Yes," he said, but she could see that his interest had waned.

"It was from the prophet Isaiah. God was talking to him about the testings he would have in the future. God told him this to encourage him to trust in Him. He said, 'When thou passest through the waters I shall be with thee and through the rivers, they shall not overflow thee.'"

"That's queer. How could that apply to me?"

"I don't know and she couldn't remember why she had quoted that verse to you. Then she said after that she sang part of a little chorus that I sing so often. She used to love to hear me sing it. I always sing it when I'm downhearted. It goes like this."

She sang the words in low reverent tones, just loud enough for him to hear.

> He's able, He's able,
> I know He's able.
> I know my Lord is able
> To carry me through.
>
> He heals the brokenhearted,
> He sets the captive free.
> He brings the dead to life again,
> And calms the troubled sea.

Her face flushed as she saw the absorbed look in his eyes while he watched her. When she had finished, he still continued to look at her until she wondered if she had done the right thing. He seemed to be aware all at once of how he was staring at her and he lowered his eyes.

"You have a lovely voice," he said in low tones.

"Oh!" she cried in confusion, "I really have no voice. I was only thinking of the words of the chorus. Don't you think it's a beautiful little song?"

He nodded. "Why do you suppose she sang that song to me?"

"I have no idea. I don't believe that dreams have any real significance today, though God often spoke to people in dreams in the past. He doesn't have to do that today, for we have His Word through which He speaks to us."

"I wish one part of that song could be true. I wish that I could believe it would be true."

She thought she knew but she asked him just the same.

"The part that says 'He sets the captive free.' If God would do that for me, I'd be willing to believe in Him."

"We can't make bargains with God," she told him. "We have to accept Him on faith and believe that what He says He will do. If you would only believe in Him and have faith to believe that what you ask of Him, He will do, He might set you free."

"That I would have to see before I could believe," he stated flatly.

She thought it best to change the subject, so she told him that Terry had promised to do what he could to have him restored as a trusty.

"You should know him better than that by now," he said. "He not only didn't do what he promised you he would do, but when the warden put in a plea for me, he was there to object. I'll never get it again, thanks to him. They gave me the honor of working in the factory," he said sarcastically.

"But he promised," she said.

"He promised!" His voice was mocking. "You're the only person I've met since I came here who ever keeps a promise."

"Then I don't suppose the other thing he told me was true."

"What was that?" he asked.

"He told me that he was no longer the executioner."

"He lied. There was an execution night before last and he was the one who pulled the switch."

"I'm going to see what I can do to undo the wrong I have done to you," she said as she saw the guard approaching.

"Please don't do it," he said under his breath as the guard came nearer. "It may hurt you if people know that you are trying to help me."

She did not answer but gave him a parting smile and told him that she would come again soon.

She was angry as well as hurt with Terry for the way he had deceived her. She had not seen him except at church for she had been staying with Mrs. Field. She decided that she would let him come to see her again if he asked for a date and then she would tell him that she knew the truth. Then she would have nothing more to do with him. She felt that he had done all the harm he could to Bill, so she need not fear that he would do anything more even though he would be more angry with Bill than ever.

She decided that she would appeal to her uncle for his

aid in trying to get Bill restored to liberty as a trusty. He knew both the warden and the sheriff. Perhaps through them she might attain her purpose.

Terry phoned soon after her visit to the prison. He knew that she had been taking care of Mrs. Field for Mrs. Barton had told him so.

When he came she lost no time in telling him what was on her mind. She was anxious to get the unpleasant interview over with as soon as possible.

"I'm sorry you didn't do what you promised to do about Bill Gordon," she said.

"But I did," he insisted. "I told you that I would do what I could, but I also told you that this was entirely out of my hands. I tried, but they turned me down. Much as I wanted to keep my word and please you, I think they did the right thing when they turned me down."

"That is not the truth, Terry," she told him. "Instead of trying to help him, it was your protest that kept him from getting his liberty."

"He told you this, of course," he said angrily. "I know that you have been coming to see him and giving him a lot of sympathy."

"He certainly needs a lot," she retorted. "He deserves sympathy from someone after the way he's been treated. If you call that justice, I don't."

"How can you take the word of that criminal against mine? It's too bad that you've let your sympathy for this fellow come between us, Meredith. Why can't you forget him and let us be friends like we were before he came along to upset things? Please believe me, he isn't worth all the trouble he's caused."

"He's worth as much in God's sight as you are," she informed him coldly. "He's a sinner and so are you."

"I'm surprised at you, Meredith," he cried angrily. "How can you let yourself go so far as to put me in the same class as that condemned murderer?"

"In God's sight you are also under condemnation and God is no respecter of persons. Bill has been condemned as a murderer but you have lied to me and tried to deceive me while you were venting your spite against someone who could not defend himself. Sin is sin in God's sight. So, in His sight, you are no better than he."

"It's good to know just where I stand with you," he said.

His face was white and he stared at her coldly.

"You also told me," she continued relentlessly, "that you had given up the job as executioner. That also is not true."

"He'll wish that he had never told you this," he said through stiff lips. "He got off easily the last time. This time it will not be so easy."

"You will do nothing more to him," she said as the cold light in her eyes held his angry glare. "If necessary, I shall go before the governor and tell him the truth. It might cost you your job if I do that."

"If you did that I wouldn't be able to finish my law course. I'm sure you wouldn't let your righteous indignation take you that far," he said, trying to be sarcastic. But she saw the uneasiness in his eyes.

"Did you stop to think of what Bill Gordon's liberty meant to him? It meant a few hours outside those prison walls. Now, if someone doesn't intercede for him, he'll have to spend the rest of his life there."

"But he deserves to be there!" Terry exploded. "You're letting your sympathy run away with your better judgment."

"I'm not sure that he is guilty," she retorted.

"Of course he told you that he was innocent. That's what they all say."

"But I happen to believe that this one told the truth. That's more than I can say about you, Terry."

His face flushed and he got to his feet.

"Let me ask you once more to reconsider this matter and think over your interfering in this," he said peremptorily.

"I have no intention of reconsidering." Her tones were adamant. "I'm sorry, but if you want me to reconsider, then you'd better do what you promised to do."

He told her good night stiffly and closed the door with a bang. If he would do what he promised to do to help that fellow! He'd see him dead first!

CHAPTER 19

MEREDITH WAS BOTH SURPRISED and touched when Mrs. Field's will was probated. The old lady had nothing but the home in which she had lived for so long, for she had been living on a pension, but she left the house and contents to Meredith, "In grateful appreciation for a friendship which meant so much to me and with the knowledge that whatever may be done with this bequest will be done for the Lord's work."

There were some antique pieces which Meredith was able to sell for a good price. The other furniture she gave to poor families who attended Mark's church. She was able to sell the house for more than she had anticipated. When she received the check for the sale, she endorsed it over to Mark.

"This will help to pay for your equipment and passage when you are ready to go to the field," she told him. "It is what she would have wanted more than anything else," she said when he hesitated to take it. "It would make her happy to know that she was helping in this way."

"I shall try to use it wisely," he told her. "How I wish that I could look forward to having you go with me!"

"How I wish you could," she echoed as she put her hand over his.

He took it and pressed it gently to his lips. He never mentioned his love for her, though she could see it in his stolen glances when he thought she did not see and she could detect it in the tone of his voice. She appreciated his tact, for she knew that he found it hard not to do as Terry had done and continue to remind her of what was uppermost in his mind when he was with her. He did not want to annoy her or to do anything which would strain their relationship in their work together.

Meredith had missed the next visiting day at the prison for she was busy settling up the sale of the house. She wondered if Bill had been expecting her and if he would think she had lost interest in him. She had hoped each time that they had held services at the prison that he would be there, but he did not come. However, on the Sunday after visiting day, when she looked over the group she saw him sitting in the last seat, almost hidden by those in front of him.

She caught his gaze fixed upon her before he realized that she had discovered him and what she saw disturbed her. It brought a sudden fluttering to her heart which disturbed her more. In the man's eyes was a look which she could not mistake.

When she caught his eye she gave him a smile. His face flushed and the shadow of a smile responded to hers, then he lowered his eyes.

During the service Meredith was praying that what the youngsters were singing and what Mark was saying would somehow reach his unbelieving heart. Mark surprised her by asking her to give her testimony.

The attendance had grown since the first few meetings and she had seen evidence of genuine interest on the part of some of the men. Mark had been able to talk with some of them on visiting days and several had been genuinely converted. They had proved it by asking for a Bible and they had been reading it in spite of ridicule or scorn from their cell mates.

Meredith told the simple story of her conversion and of what salvation meant to her, not only in bringing joy and peace each day but in giving her strength and victory over temptation and grief. She told them of Mrs. Field's life and how much the old lady's friendship had meant to her. She told them of how her going had grieved her, yet how she rejoiced because the old lady had been happy over the thought that she was going home.

The men listened with rapt attention and she saw signs of a struggle going on in the hearts of some as she watched their faces. She glanced at Bill and saw that his face was white and strained and he was looking at her as a drowning man might look at one who stood ready to save him. She could feel the struggle that was going on within him and she prayed as she spoke, that some of his doubt and bitterness would disappear and that he might open his heart to the pleading of the Holy Spirit.

When the service was ended he left without looking at her and her hope grew dim. Little did either of them realize how soon Bill would need the comfort and hope which God alone could give.

It was not long after this that tragedy struck, swiftly and unexpectedly. It plunged Bill into the depths of despair and brought Meredith to the greatest trial her faith had ever yet encountered.

There had been trouble brewing for some time at the prison, a secret feud between two of the prisoners, Sam Martin and Tony Farrow. Sam had sworn to get even with Bill Gordon because he had suspected Bill of his part in quelling the budding riot some months previous. Bill was aware of this, but he could do nothing but be on his guard. He could not go to the warden with his suspicions for he knew that Terry might cause more trouble for him if he did that. In the meantime Tony and Sam became bitter enemies over some quarrel of their own. The prisoners began to take sides and it might have ended in another riot, but something happened which brought a sudden end to the quarrel but which plunged Bill into the midst of tragedy.

The prisoners were returning from their work in the prison factory where Bill and the two had been working near each other. Tony and Sam were the last in line while Bill was detained a few minutes by the foreman. As he rounded a corner, hurrying to catch up with the others, so that he would not be reprimanded for not being in line, he saw Sam lying on the floor with a knife in his back.

He stared in horror at the still form, wondering even in that brief moment how anyone could have gotten that knife and how it could have happened so quickly without causing any commotion. He bent down to see whether or not Sam was dead and he did a fatal thing. He drew the knife from Sam's body and held it in his hand while he felt for the fallen man's pulse. Sam was really dead.

Just then a voice called him and held him petrified with the sudden horrifying realization of what he had let himself in for. It was Terry's voice.

"Stay where you are," his cold voice commanded. "There's no doubt about this murder. I've caught you in the very act."

"I didn't kill him!" Bill cried. "Someone else did it. I was trying to see if he was dead."

"On your feet," Terry commanded. "And drop that knife. Of course you didn't do it. Just as you didn't commit that other murder. This time you'll go to the chair. You won't escape, for I shall testify against you."

There was gloating in his eyes and a faint smile of satisfaction upon his lips. Bill could see how glad the other was that at last he had him where he could not escape and it roused him to uncontrolled fury. Once more this man would do all in his power to make him suffer for something which he had not done. He struck out with all his force in blind rage and sent Terry sprawling. Terry cried out for a guard, but one was already coming toward them, for Bill and Sam were not in line.

The guard jerked Bill to one side and held a gun against his ribs. He was marched back to his cell followed by Terry, once more nursing a swollen jaw. The door opened and Bill was pushed into his cell and the door clanged shut. The lock was turned and Bill was left to await a fate which he felt was only too certain. This time, as Terry had threatened, he would not escape.

He sank upon the bunk and beat his fists against his head. What a fool he had been to have begun to believe that there was a God! She had made God so real in her talk while such faith and utter peace had radiated from her as she told them of the love of God that he had almost begun to believe. What rot! There was no God and there was no justice. If there was, then why was that smug hypocrite allowed to go unpunished while he had been condemned for something of which he had not been guilty?

He knew the one who had committed that murder would never confess for he had an idea that it was Tony. He also knew that the others, if they had witnessed the crime, would never expose Tony. If they did, they might meet with the same fate from one of Tony's friends. Better to let an innocent man pay the penalty for this crime than for themselves to be in danger of being murdered just as Sam had been.

He knew that indeed there was no way of escape this time. Terry would see to that and he would be glad to be rid of someone who had struck him twice and brought reprimand upon him for neglect of duty in the past. How he would smirk and say that the law must be upheld and that one more criminal had paid the penalty he deserved to get. A criminal who was no better than a savage beast!

CHAPTER **20**

THE NEWSPAPERS CARRIED THE STORY of the murder and played it up in headlines. The opposing political faction saw an opportunity to use it to their advantage. Election time was approaching and this might help them to defeat the other party. It would be an added proof of what they claimed was the inefficiency of the present prison management. The paper demanded an immediate trial of the murderer, claiming that in the past too many had escaped just punishment for their crimes by long delayed trials.

Meredith read the news with increasing horror. She knew that Bill would stand little chance this time to escape death. His former crime would be held against him and this time there would be no doubt about his guilt, for Terry had witnessed the murder. The paper emphasized the fact there must be some laxity in prison management which allowed a prisoner to gain possession of the knife that had killed Sam.

Meredith was heartsick over the situation. She had had such hopes for Bill and now those hopes had been destroyed completely. She went to see Bill but she was told that he could not see anyone until he was brought before the grand jury.

She waited nervously for the verdict of the grand jury, hoping against hope that Bill would not be indicted for murder. While she waited and tried to hope, she prayed.

The verdict was announced quickly. Bill was charged with murder and his trial was set for an early date.

Meredith went to her uncle. She wanted to see Bill and she wanted to see him alone. She could not help but feel that if she talked with him, he might give her some hope that he was not guilty.

"Please go to Mr. Harris and try to persuade him to let me talk to Bill Gordon somewhere besides that awful visitors' room," she begged. "I'm sure he won't refuse you."

"Why do you want to see this man?" her uncle asked. "Are you going to be like those other silly women? As soon as someone gets into trouble like this, they get morbidly sympathetic and worry the warden as well as the prisoner by cooing over him and telling him how sorry they feel for him. I've heard Harris say, 'Just let me get a new murderer in here and I'll be besieged by a horde of sob sisters.' "

"You know I'm not like that," Meredith reproved him. "But I must talk to this man. I know him and he has no one else who cares what happens to him."

"You know him!" her uncle exploded. "How did this ever happen?"

She explained how she had first met Bill and told him how he had incurred Terry's wrath and the consequences. She told him of the time when the truck had overturned and Mrs. Field had taken him into her home. She did not tell him of the times she had met him and talked to him about his soul, for she knew that he would not understand and she feared that he might misunderstand her motives.

She could not understand her own feelings now. She was desperately concerned about his soul, but she could not forget the look she had discovered in his eyes. It worried her, for she could not understand her own feelings when she remembered that look which she had seen more than once in his eyes and when she realized Bill's dangerous situation now.

Mr. Barton promised to do what he could and he went to see the warden. Mr. Harris refused to grant Meredith's request for he felt the criticism of his opponents keenly. He had faithfully performed his duties as warden and he knew that his political foes knew this also.

Mr. Barton went to the sheriff and from there he spoke to a friend who was a member of the Mayor's council and his request was finally granted.

When Meredith went to see Bill she was taken into the small room adjoining the warden's office. The guard brought Bill in and stood outside looking through the glass in the upper part of the door. This was the precaution taken so that there would be no chance for a weapon to be slipped to the prisoner. The two chairs were facing each other and were in direct line of the guard's vision.

Bill sat down and faced her silently. His face was white and drawn and his eyes were clouded and hopeless, as if he had already looked into the future and saw what was waiting for him at the end of the road.

"I came as soon as I could get permission," she said.

"Why bother to come at all?" he replied. He gave her a brief glance, then turned his eyes away.

"Because I want to help you," she said earnestly.

"No one can help me now," he said wearily.

She could see by the deep circles under his eyes that he had not slept much and she could sense the fear underneath his outward calmness. A great ache filled her heart and a surge of sympathy swept over her. How terror-stricken she would be if she were in his place and did not have the comfort that God alone could give! Only He could take away the fear of death and she knew that Bill must be dying a thousand deaths as he looked forward to the trial. She knew he felt that there was no way of escape, and, as far as she could see, there was no way out. But she had cried aloud to the Lord to whom she had turned many times and who had never failed her in the past, that He would find a way if Bill was not guilty. She had come here today in the hope of getting another version of the murder from him, though that hope was faint.

"God can help you, Bill," she said quietly but with conviction.

"God!" he spat the word out with bitter contempt. "What does He care what happens to me? If there is a God, He would never have let this happen. If there is a God, He has forgotten that I exist."

"That's not true, Bill. Jesus Himself said that not a sparrow falls to the ground without God's notice. He said you are worth much more to Him, for His Son died to save you from your sin. If you'd only believe, He could help you even now, if you're not guilty. Even if you are, He can save your soul if you'd only ask Him."

"You too think I'm guilty, don't you?" he cried as his eyes pierced hers.

"Not if you say you're not," she said gently.

His look melted and his lip trembled in spite of his effort to steady it.

"Do you mean that?" he asked. There was pleading mingled with doubt and hope in his voice.

"Yes, I do. That is why I was so determined to see you alone. I couldn't talk out there with all that noise and with so little time. Tell me what happened. I shall believe what you tell me."

"You're so wonderful!" he said under his breath. "If I had only known you long ago perhaps I could have believed as you do. How I wish I could!"

"Tell me what happened," she said, coloring under his look and the tone of his whispered voice which shook with suppressed emotion.

He told her what happened and emphasized Terry's gloating words which made him so angry that he struck Terry and knocked him down.

"He lied when he said that he saw the murder," he told her. "When he came around the corner, the man was already dead and all he saw was me kneeling there by the body with the knife in my hand. I had foolishly pulled it out of Sam's body. I didn't realize what a trap I was falling into until he accused me of killing the man."

"But surely he'll tell the truth when he takes the witness stand," she said, trying to give him some hope.

She knew that the blow he had given Terry would react unfavorably upon the minds of the jury, especially if Terry told about that other blow Bill had given him.

"He won't. He'll be only too glad to perjure himself to see me get what he thought I deserved long ago. He'll even pull the lever that will send me to my death. He'll convince himself that he's doing his righteous duty to a criminal who is little better than a savage beast."

Meredith saw his face turn whiter at the mention of the electric chair and her own heart almost stopped beating at the thought. Once before he had faced this terrible possibility, but now it would be a certainty.

"It can't happen! It must not happen!" she cried in distress. "I believe that you are innocent and I shall pray that in some way God will save you. Surely He cannot fail to answer all the prayers and tears I have offered up for you."

"Does it matter that much to you?" he asked.

"Yes, it does. I've prayed for your soul ever since that first day I met you. No matter how impossible it may seem to you, I still believe that God is able not only to save your soul but to deliver you. I know that the prayer of a believer avails much. I remember the words of one of my favorite choruses. 'God is able.' Remember how Mrs. Field sang them to you in her dream? 'He sets the captive free.' I still believe that He can do that just as He opened the prison doors for Peter and for Paul. That means physically as well as spiritually."

He was silent a moment, then he said, "She said something about passing through waters. Do you think she could have meant this?"

"I'm sure she didn't know what it meant, but perhaps God did," she told him. "Those words are true, so whether the dream meant anything or not, just try to believe those words and try to hope. I shall pray and I shall do all in my power to help you."

The guard tapped on the door to let them know that they had talked long enough. Bill rose and gave her a smile.

"How I thank you for coming!" he said. "You will never know what it has meant to me, just knowing you."

She returned his smile and watched him go through the door, but there was an ache in her heart and a desperate prayer that God would indeed be with him while he was passing through these deep waters.

She prayed as she went out of the prison and on her way home and then on her knees in her room, that Bill would be able to claim that promise before it was too late. But her faith was weak and she prayed for the increase of the faith which alone would bring peace to her aching heart.

CHAPTER **21**

THOUGH THE NEWSPAPER AND THE opposing political element had obtained their demand for an early trial, it was delayed longer than they had anticipated. So much publicity had been given to the case that it was proving difficult to select a jury.

Justice demanded that an impartial jury should try the case, but when Meredith saw the twelve men who were finally sworn in, she did not have any hope that they would acquit Bill. They were not the type to harbor any thought of mercy. Their faces were hard and they showed that they were upset over having to be away from their jobs. They would be impatient to get the trial over with, no matter what the verdict might be.

The court had appointed a lawyer for Bill, but she knew that this was only a form and that this man would not spend himself to prove his client innocent. It would be just a farce like the other one Bill had told her about. What chance would he have for a plea for clemency when there was already another charge of murder against him? Even before the trial had gotten well under way she could see that the jury had already condemned him in their minds.

She was there on the opening day of the trial, sitting as near Bill as she could get. She had asked Mark to go with her and he sat beside her while the trial drew to its swift close. She knew that Mark shared her interest and sympathy for Bill but he could not know the depth of her pain as she watched Bill's stolid face, now pale and drawn, but with eyes that did not waver as he watched those who took the witness stand.

Once she caught his eye and gave him a smile, but there was no answering smile upon his lips. The look he gave her told her how utterly hopeless he was.

A couple of the prisoners who were just ahead of Sam were called but they swore that they did not see or hear anything. This could have been possible, for it was evident that Sam died without a sound, for the knife pierced his heart and, directed by a skillful hand, it could have struck so swiftly that those in front of Sam might not have been aware of what was happening.

Meredith could not help but feel that these men were perjuring themselves to protect the real murderer as well as to protect themselves. She was familiar with the prison code, the unwritten law against "squealing" on a pal and that of swift revenge upon anyone who did. She was sure that these men knew who had killed Sam.

Tony was brought to the stand and questioned by the prosecuting attorney, but the questions he put to the fellow were perfunctory and asked as if he were merely fulfilling the requirements of the law. When Tony was cross examined by the defense lawyer, the lawyer's questions were put so indifferently that Meredith had to restrain herself from crying out in protest. He was not even halfway trying to connect Tony with the murder even though Tony confessed that he and Sam had had some differences in the past. Tony swore that this had been patched up and that they had become friends. The other prisoners had testified that this was true and the lawyer let it pass without the grilling he should have given Tony. Tony said that he was not next to Sam when they left the shop. Meredith was sure that this was not the truth, for Bill had told her that Tony was next to Sam in the line and that he himself was behind them.

"They're railroading him," she whispered to Mark as Tony left the stand with a look of relief on his rat-like face.

"They've convicted him already," he replied.

"And they call this justice!" she cried bitterly in a tense low voice while she tried to smother a sob. "How I wish I could help him!"

"Let's not give up hope," he said, trying to encourage her. "Remember, God is still able."

"Yes, but I wonder if He is willing. Bill has scoffed and doubted for so long. He's come so near to blaspheming that perhaps God has left him to his fate."

"He has said that He is long suffering, not willing that any should perish, but that all should come to everlasting life," Mark reminded her.

"But He has also said 'My Spirit shall not always strive with man.' Perhaps Bill has missed his last chance. If I could only make him see what eternity without Christ will be!"

Bill was called to the stand and Meredith waited tensely for him to testify in his own behalf. This time the prosecuting attorney threw questions at him like pistol shots, harsh and merciless, scarcely giving him time to answer one before he threw another at him. There was no protest from Bill's lawyer when some of the questions should have been challenged.

What a farce this was! Bill was already convicted, no matter what his testimony might reveal. He told the court with much difficulty, for the lawyer continued to pelt him with questions, of how he had been detained in the shop and of how he had found Sam's body just a few minutes after the line had turned the corner, of how he had pulled the knife out and held it while he tried to see if Sam was really dead.

The lawyer produced the knife and testified that there were no other finger prints on the murder weapon but those of Bill's. So, Meredith decided, if Tony was the killer, he must have worn gloves. Bill left the stand without being questioned by his lawyer. Then Terry was called to the stand.

Meredith watched him closely as he took his seat, but Terry refused to meet her eyes, though she was sitting directly in front of him. The prosecuting attorney asked leading questions and Terry told the court how he had seen Bill come around the corner and catch up with Sam. He said that he had seen Bill produce the knife and strike Sam with a blow that dropped him to the floor without a sound or struggle.

"That's a lie and he knows it's a lie!" Bill cried as he half rose from his chair.

Two policemen standing nearby shoved him roughly back into his chair. He sat there slumped over with his head in his hands. He knew that he had only made it worse for himself by his outburst and he listened without moving to Terry reciting the incident of being struck down by him. Even before the case was closed, he knew what the verdict would be.

Meredith wondered how the judge could sit through this farce without interrupting and trying to bring at least some pretense of justice into the trial, but she knew only too well that he, as well as everyone else, thought Bill was a hardened murderer and deserved death. The story of that former crime had been publicized and those who might have had a shred of sympathy for him were now willing to see him pay the supreme penalty, for they felt that it was long overdue.

It did not take long for the jury to return with their verdict. During the brief interval Bill had been taken into another room to wait for the jury to return. Meredith sat waiting tensely. Every nerve in her body seemed to ache with the tension and with sympathy for Bill. She could imagine what he must be suffering, now doubly so, for he had passed through this same ordeal before. Before there had been a faint hope. Now, however, she was sure he must know that there was none.

When he was brought in, with every eye upon him, he glanced across to where she sat. In his eyes there was that same brief glimpse of agony that she had seen there when she had talked with him at their last interview. Quick tears came to her eyes. He saw them and he looked away, but she saw his chin quiver suspiciously for an instant, then he braced himself and took his place waiting for the judge's order to stand. It came and he stood with shoulders squared and head uplifted and with eyes fastened upon the judge. He listened while the brief words of his doom were spoken, death in the electric chair, the date to be set by the court.

Amid the subdued hum of voices he was led from the room. He had not winced when the verdict was pronounced, but had stood stolidly while his eyes bored so piercingly into the eyes of the judge that the judge was forced to turn his gaze away. He walked with steady stride through the door and out of sight.

"He's sure a hardened specimen," someone nearby remarked.

Meredith turned blazing eyes upon the one who had made that remark. He wasn't a hardened specimen, he was a man who had lost hope and was facing death stolidly. While tears blinded her eyes, she let Mark lead her from the room.

CHAPTER 22

WHEN THE TRIAL OF BILL GORDON had ended with his conviction, the public lost interest and only those immediately connected with the case waited with varying emotions for the day of execution.

The court had fixed the date of the execution for two months later. The district attorney was mildly surprised that the time was so long delayed. However, since the trial was over and his part in the farce had not been publicly criticized, he had no more interest in the case. The verdict had been rendered and one more criminal would be out of the way, with no further expense to the state. He could turn his attention to other matters, the forthcoming election and his own future political career.

The warden realized that his position was in danger, for the attack of the papers had been directed against him with vitriolic accusations. He knew that these charges were without foundation, but the paper which was owned by his political foes was using all the power of the press to have him ousted after the coming election. He had faithfully performed his duties and he had given the men in his charge something which they had not known before, sympathy and understanding even while he was being just and doing his duty to see that prison rules were obeyed.

He had felt sorry for Bill from the beginning of his imprisonment and his sympathy for him had grown during the years. He had had enough experience with prisoners to recognize the difference between the hardened type who committed crimes either for revenge or hatred or the desire for easy living through stolen money, or the degenerate type who committed crimes through the lust which ruled their distorted natures. He knew the difference between these types and the fellow who had been led into crime and had made his first fatal mistake. He knew that, no matter how carefully the law might operate to see that justice was accorded everyone who came under its judgment, mistakes were sometimes made, sometimes when it was too late to remedy the mistake.

When Bill was committed to prison, though he came as a convicted robber and murderer, Harris could not help but feel sorry for him. Bill did not impress him as a person who could do the thing for which he had been convicted. He knew that he could not always judge by appearances, and he could not account for his strong sympathy, but he had a vague intuition which made him feel that somewhere, somehow, justice must have been blind. Because of this, he watched him, perhaps, more closely than many of the other prisoners under his charge.

He noted with regret how morose and bitter Bill became during the years he was in prison, but he realized that there was sufficient reason for that. Other prisoners, even though they were in for life, had the hope, however faint, of one day being eligible for parole, while some had hopes of being pardoned. Bill, however, had been sentenced without any hope of either parole or pardon. He must live out his life behind prison bars and that lifetime would be long, for he was only twenty-four when he was committed.

The warden observed that, though he was bitter and morose, he was a model prisoner, keeping the rules faithfully and willing to help whenever there was need of it beyond what he was compelled to do. When Bill discovered the plot to incite a riot which, if the plans had been carried out, would perhaps have resulted in many deaths, and had been the indirect means of stopping it, Harris was glad to do what he could to have the rules set aside in order that Bill might be made a trusty.

Mr. Harris felt sure that Bill was innocent of this second crime, though of course he had no proof. He still felt this even when Terry testified that he had seen Bill kill Sam. He felt that Tony was the guilty one. He was aware of the feud between Tony and Sam and he knew that Tony was relentless in his hatred and desire for revenge. Tony would be glad to have Bill convicted for the crime, for this would satisfy a desire for revenge upon Bill for having betrayed their plot to incite the riot. Both he and Sam had suspected Bill of betraying them. They had been the instigators of the plot though it had never been proven against them. With Bill out of the way, he would have had his revenge upon both of his enemies.

Mr. Harris questioned Terry about his testimony with such persistence that Terry turned upon his uncle in anger and threatened to accuse him of trying to thwart justice.

"You've shown partiality to that murderer ever since he came here," Terry cried. "I saw it as soon as I came here. If the papers knew this they would make it much hotter for you than they have done. You'd lose your job, no matter which party won the election."

Mr. Harris had learned much about his nephew in the last few months and what he had learned was not good. Though he was highly thought of in the community as a young man with every good quality and with a bright future, his uncle saw him for what he was, a narrow-minded, self-righteous individual with love for no one but himself and with a nature which harbored revenge and spite as strongly as those of like type who were behind bars.

Even though he knew Terry for what he was, Terry's threat hurt him, for he had helped his nephew when he needed help most. When the family fortune had suddenly taken wings through an unwise investment of Terry's father, Mr. Harris had given him the position as his deputy while he was finishing his law course.

"What would happen to you if I should lose my position?" he asked coldly. But there was sadness in his eyes.

"It would not matter much," Terry retorted. "By the time the new administration should take over if they should win, I would have enough ahead to tide me over until I could get established."

"Including the money you will receive from the execution of Bill Gordon," his uncle said sternly.

Terry's face went white.

"Why are you so chicken-hearted about that fellow?" he blazed. "He's a murderer twice over, yet you've made him a sort of teacher's pet."

Harris looked him squarely in the eye as he clipped out the words slowly and forcefully, "I don't believe that Bill Gordon killed Sam."

He held Terry's eyes until Terry was forced to shift his gaze and in that moment he was convinced that his nephew had perjured himself.

"You've hated that man for a long time," Harris continued. "You're taking a terrible way to get your revenge."

"I refuse to discuss this further," Terry stormed. "If I let you go on much longer, you'll be saying that I killed Sam. Bill Gordon was convicted by a court of justice and under the law he must die. If the law had done its duty in the first place, he would have been dead long ago."

He turned and walked out, slamming the door behind him, leaving his uncle with a great weight upon his heart and a sense of futility to avert that which he felt to be a horrible miscarriage of justice. His hands were tied. He could do nothing but pray. He was a praying man. Religion was a vital factor in his life, not just a cloak of righteousness worn to create respect. That was the one thing which had helped him in his dealings with the prisoners. It had helped him to rehabilitate more than one young man who had been caught in the net of crime, and who had gone out to live a decent life and to thank him for his part in making that possible.

Meredith tried not to let her aunt and uncle know how depressed and grieved she was and how she dreaded the passing of each day, for each day brought the time of Bill's execution that much nearer. Her efforts, however, were not successful, for they saw how unhappy she was and they guessed the reason.

"Why do you let yourself worry so over that man?" her

aunt asked her one day at lunch when Meredith only nibbled and pretended to eat.

"I can't help it, Aunt Mary," Meredith said. "I keep thinking that in a little while he will go out into eternity a lost soul."

"That's no reason for you to grieve as you are doing. You act as if he were some relative. You did what you could to help him and there is nothing more that you can do. You should try to forget him."

"How can I forget him when I believe he is innocent!" Meredith cried. "I don't believe he killed that convict. I believe they are going to execute an innocent man."

"Why, Meredith!" her aunt exclaimed in surprise. "How can you think he's innocent when Terry testified that he saw the actual murder?"

"I believe he could be mistaken," Meredith said stubbornly.

"How could he be mistaken when he saw it with his very own eyes? You wouldn't accuse Terry of swearing to something that wasn't true, would you? That would be a terrible thing to accuse him of, Meredith."

"I'm not accusing anyone," Meredith said wearily. "I just know how I feel. I feel that Bill is innocent and I hate to see him die feeling so rebellious toward God." She rose to leave the room.

"I can't understand you," her aunt sighed. "The way you've been moping around here ever since the trial, one would think that you were in love with that man."

Meredith turned to her aunt with wide eyes and parted lips, in speechless surprise. Mrs. Barton came over and put her arm around Meredith and patted her cheek.

"Forgive me, dear, I didn't mean that," she said soothingly. "But I do wish that you could snap out of this. If you don't, you'll be sick. You haven't eaten a decent meal since that trial."

"I'll try, Aunt Mary." She smiled wanly into her aunt's anxious eyes before she went to her room.

She sat by the window and looked out upon the garden, warm and green under the spring sun. Birds were twittering in the trees as they busied themselves preparing their nests for the new families which would be emerging from tiny eggs not many weeks from now.

The bleak winter garden was giving promise of the wealth of blossoms soon to burst from their swelling buds on bushes that were now decked in new spring garments of bright green.

As she looked down upon the well-kept lawn and the garden soon to be ablaze with color, the dismal thought weighed upon her that when these flowers burst into bloom, Bill would be lying in an unmarked grave. And his soul would be forever in the darkness of eternal night. She dropped her head upon her hands on the window sill and let the tears flow. She had failed miserably and she had tried so hard. She had won many to the Lord but she had failed in this one effort and, in the light of that failure, all the other victories seemed of no worth. She tried to pray, but for a long while she could not.

She had prayed earnestly for some miracle that would prove Bill's innocence but her prayer had not been answered and now it seemed that her faith could not reach through the gloom of her grief and despair. But as her tears subsided and she struggled for words, she prayed humbly for faith to believe God's promise to hear and answer prayer. But prayer, she remembered, must be in the will of God. Even this prayer of intercession must be in His will.

How could this be otherwise than God's will, she argued to herself when she had finished praying. Wasn't she praying for the soul of a man who would soon be sent into eternity? And hadn't God's Word said that it was not His will for anyone to perish?

She could find no answer to her own arguments. She bowed her head again and prayed that she might be in God's will, but before she had finished, she once more uttered the petition which she had asked many times before during this terrible time, that somehow God would perform a miracle and save Bill from death if he was not guilty.

"If he is guilty, O God, please give me the chance to win his soul for Thee before he goes to his death," she sobbed.

She tried to talk to Bill about his soul in the few brief visits which she was allowed, but she saw that she was only making it harder for them both. The time was drawing so near that he could think of nothing but the approaching end and it was hard to talk to him through the bars while the guard stood near.

"Just remember that I shall be praying for you," she whispered before she left him. "I shall never give up hope that in some way God will intervene. I still don't believe that you are guilty."

"You're kind," he said in dull tones. All the bitterness seemed buried beneath the hopelessness of despair.

She could see how haggard he was. She knew that he was trying desperately not to show the fear that must possess every man in the face of death, everyone who was not sure of the presence of the Good Shepherd who would be there to take one through the valley of the shadow and lead him without fear into the Light beyond the valley.

When she left him a few days before the execution, she knew that she would be allowed to see him for just a few minutes the next time she came and that this would be the last. Her heart contracted with sudden pain and it was all that she could do to keep the tears back as she followed the guard down the corridor.

She had been faithful in her attendance with Mark at the services in the prison and she sang with the youngsters with a smile on her face though her heart was heavy. Mark realized the strain of these days and he was sympathetic, though he said no word except to remind her occasionally that he was praying with her.

"It seems hopeless," she said one afternoon as the time drew near. "I've prayed and prayed, but I don't seem to get any assurance of an answer."

"Do I have to remind you, Meredith, that God is able?" he asked.

"He is able, but is He willing?" she asked dismally.

"Our part is to pray and believe and then leave the answer in His hands."

"What would I do without you?" she asked, saying

what she had said many times before, while she gave him a smile.

Mark observed a new man in the audience at the prison one afternoon. He slipped into a corner and sat there with stolid face while Mark gave them a stirring message on the power of God to save and the penalty which justice demanded for refusal to accept the gift of salvation and eternal life in Christ. As he continued, he painted a vivid picture of eternity without Christ, of the eternal penalty man would pay for sin if that sin was not wiped out by the atoning blood of Christ. He had never given a message just like this before, for he knew how the average criminal mocked at sermons on "hell fire" and how they rebelled against it, but something prompted him to give this message this afternoon. He contrasted this with the love of God who had sent His Son to pay the penalty for man's sin on the Cross and who had died in man's place so that man might not have to pay the penalty for his own sin.

"A man may escape the death penalty for his crime here on earth, for man made laws and human judges can sometimes make mistakes. No court is infallible. But the crime that is not atoned for in this life through the blood of Christ when He grants forgiveness, will surely meet justice and judgment and eternal punishment. Death here on earth for crime is short, no matter how it may be administered through the law, but eternal death is long and eternal suffering is greater than man's imagination can conceive."

As he continued, then gave a brief plea for them to come to God and seek pardon, he noticed this new prisoner with his rat-like face. His halfhearted interest had vanished. He leaned forward with white face and harrowed gaze fixed intently upon Mark while he listened with parted lips as if he would not miss a word. When the call for raised hands was made, he hesitated as if he would raise his, then he slumped back dejectedly and dropped his head. When the group left the room Mark turned to Meredith.

"Did you see that new fellow in the back?" he asked. "I was almost sure that he was going to raise his hand, but he changed his mind. I was disappointed."

"Don't you know who that was?" Meredith asked. "That was Tony. Bill believes that he's the one who killed Sam. I'd never forget that face."

"I remember him now. That man was under conviction," Mark stated firmly. "I know the signs too well."

"If he really did kill Sam, perhaps he knew he'd have to confess the truth if he raised his hand."

"I hope he'll come again. He surely needs the Lord and he was undergoing a struggle this afternoon."

"What does it matter whether he comes or not?" she said indifferently. She was thinking that in just a few days Bill would die.

Mark looked at her in surprise. She had never before displayed indifference where a lost soul was concerned. Then he remembered what she must be thinking and his heart went out in sympathy for her.

Tony did not come to the next meeting. He was in the city hospital fighting a losing battle for his life, following a hemorrhage.

CHAPTER 23

THE WARDEN NOTICED THE INCREASING nervousness that Terry exhibited as the day for execution approached. Though Terry tried to conceal it, it was only too apparent to the keen eyes of his uncle. The man's face was pale and he grew thinner and when he was examining papers in the office, his hand shook, something which was a sure sign of the upset state of his mind. All of his usual calm air of superiority and self-assertiveness had forsaken him. He seldom had anything to say to his uncle and never lingered longer in the office than he had to in order to transact necessary business.

Terry had stopped attending church services. He had gone a few times after Bill's conviction, but he had not been able to meet Meredith's cold accusing eyes when their glances met during the service. He had tried to speak to her after the service the first time they met after the trial, but her greeting was so cold and formal that he did not have the courage to try again. He knew that she was avoiding him and he suffered under her coldness, for he still loved her with a passion which he could not conquer, even though he felt that there was no hope for him.

He tried to tell himself that, perhaps, after the whole affair was over and she could have time to forget about the part he had played in it, there might be hope for him, but he knew that he was only trying to fool himself and that it would never be true. He saw her so constantly with Mark that he feared she might be in love with Mark. But, he admitted disconsolately, whether she was or not, there was little hope for himself. He held Bill responsible for the rift and his hatred for Bill remained with him even though his dread of the approaching execution increased with every passing day.

The day before the fatal day he went to his uncle and asked to be released from his duty as executioner.

"Why this sudden reluctance to do your job?" the warden asked. "It has paid you well and you've been satisfied with it until now. You've admitted that it helped out on your law course. Have you forgotten that you asked for the job?"

"I haven't forgotten anything," Terry replied angrily. "But I feel that, since I was chief witness at the trial, someone else should take over. It doesn't seem fair. I feel that I shouldn't be the one to send him to his death when it was my testimony that brought about his conviction."

His uncle emitted a short mirthless ejaculation.

"You should be the logical one because of that. Your conscience has suddenly grown tender. Why should it matter who pulls that switch? You'll only be fulfilling the law. Didn't you say just recently that he should have been put to death long ago? You will only be fulfilling a long-delayed demand of justice."

Terry heard the bitter sarcasm in his uncle's voice and he knew well that his uncle had seen through his hypocrisy and that the warden despised him.

"No matter what I said then, I've changed my mind about doing this particular job. I don't want to do it and I'm asking you to release me."

"Is it because you know that you lied at the trial?" Mr. Harris probed while his eyes bored into Terry's.

"No! Of course not!" Terry cried loudly. "You know that that would be perjury. Why should I do a thing like that?"

"I've known men to do worse things than that because of their hatred for a person. You wouldn't be the first person who had sent a man to his death because of that very thing. You know that as well as I do."

"How dare you even think that about me?" Terry cried furiously. "I've told you the reason I want to be replaced."

"There is no time for that now," the warden informed him coldly. "I paid for your training as an electrician so that you could take this job. I couldn't get anyone to replace you on this short notice. It's up to you."

"Well, I won't do it!" Terry's voice rose hysterically. "You'll either get someone else or let the job wait until you can."

"You'll do it or you'll wish you had!" The warden's voice was cold but harsh and Terry quailed before the look in his eyes. "You're not going to play the coward now. You were brave when you were on that witness stand condemning a man to death with your testimony. Now you'll finish the job or I'll demand that the court reopen the case on the premise that you perjured yourself at that trial. I'll make it so hot for you that you'll wish you had never heard the name of Bill Gordon. If you're not put in prison for what you did, you'll never be able to practice law or to live in this town."

Terry stood speechless before the white-hot wrath of the man facing him.

"You're just bluffing," he finally managed to say.

"Try me and see," his uncle retorted. "I can't prove anything, but I can think a lot and I think you're sending an innocent man to his death."

He knew that he was bluffing, for there was not sufficient evidence for a reopening of the case.

"He's already a convicted murderer," Terry said weakly. His face was white and his eyes were filled with terror.

"That has nothing to do with this case and you know it," Mr. Harris retorted. "Now get out of here and let me finish this report. And you be here on time tomorrow or take the consequences."

Terry walked from the room with shaky step. Looking after him, his uncle was almost sorry for him. No longer was he the arrogant son of an aristocratic family and a respected member of the church board. He was a broken man with a great fear in his heart. Mr. Harris wondered how he would stand the strain of what he must do tomorrow.

He turned to his desk but he found it difficult to concentrate. He could not keep his mind off thoughts of Bill Gordon waiting so stolidly and so hopelessly in the death cell and the white-faced Terry who had slumped through the door. He tried to pray, but he found it difficult to pray. He didn't know just how to pray in this crisis or what to pray for. He could only pray if Bill was innocent, that in some way he would be saved from a terrible death.

The day of execution dawned gloomy and cloudy, with a steady rain soaking the earth and adding gloom to hearts already weighed down by sorrow and despair.

It was allowed to the nearest relative of the prisoner to visit him before the end and, since Bill had no near relative, Meredith had asked for this privilege. When she saw him, her heart was so full that she could not speak for a moment, but just looked at him while tears which she could not restrain filled her eyes and overflowed upon her pale cheeks.

"It was good of you to come," Bill said in a husky voice, breaking the awkward silence.

"I wanted to come," she said trying to keep her voice steady. "Oh, Bill! How I wish that I could say something that would make you see that God loves you and wants to save your soul! I can't bear to think of you going out into eternity without salvation."

"How can I believe that God loves me when He lets me die for something that I didn't do?" he cried in agonized tones. "I've tried to believe what you tell me, for I know that you have something that I don't have, but how can I have faith to believe when everything that could happen against me has happened? If there is a God and if He loves me, how could He let all this happen?"

"I don't know," she said as a sob choked her. "I've prayed for you every day that God would give you faith to believe. All my life I shall be sorry, oh, so sorry, because I failed you."

"You didn't fail me," he said as a warm note crept into his voice. "Knowing you has been the one bright spot in my life since I came here. If I had known you before this happened, perhaps I would have believed."

He had said this before, but now there was a new note in

his voice which arrested her tears as she looked at him.

"I want to tell you something that I never dared to say before," he continued. "Now it will not matter, for I'll soon be gone and it can't hurt you. I love you. I've loved you ever since that first day when you tried so hard to convince me that there was a God and that He cared for me. My love for you has kept me through days when it seemed that I couldn't go on. It kept me from killing myself when there was no other incentive to live. I wanted to live just so that I could see you again and hear your voice. I love you, Meredith, my darling. It can't hurt you now for me to call you that or to tell you how much I love you."

She looked at him through her tears with parted lips. She could not speak, for the words seemed choked in her throat.

"Are you angry because I told you?" he asked as she remained silent.

"Oh, no. I'm not angry," she stammered. "I — I — just don't know what to say."

The guard approached to tell her that her time was up and she turned in distress to Bill.

"What can I say, Bill? What can I say?" she cried. "If there were only something that I could do!"

"There is something that you can do," he said gravely. "Would you grant one last request of a man who is about to die?" He looked at her anxiously.

"Yes, of course, if I can," she told him.

"Will you let me kiss you, just once? I know I have no right to ask it, but it's the one thing that I want, just the touch of your lips. Will you, Meredith? Please!"

She hesitated a moment while the guard stood at one side waiting, then she said, "Yes, Bill, I will."

She held up her tear-wet face to his and he kissed her gently, then looked for a moment into her eyes so near his own.

"Thank you!" he murmured and his lip trembled. "I shall carry this memory with me until the end."

She turned away, blinded by tears. Mark was waiting for her as she left him and together they went out into the gloomy spring day. They got into his car and drove slowly from the grim gray building down the road over which Meredith had once traveled with such a light heart and with a song upon her lips. The memory of that song came to her now. "He is able, He is able."

Suddenly she burst into tears and sobbed without restraint.

Mark stopped the car at the side of the road and put his arm around her. She let her head rest upon his shoulder while the tears flowed.

"Just cry all you want to," he said comfortingly. "It will help you. You've been in such a nervous strain all these long weeks."

"Oh Mark, I can't bear it! I can't bear it!" she moaned between sobs.

"God will help you, dear," he murmured as he stroked her hair. "I know how hard it is for you because you love him."

She raised her head and looked at him while the sobs suddenly ceased.

"Because I love him!" she echoed. "Why did you say that?"

He smiled into her tear-filled eyes.

"I've known it for some time."

"It's true," she said slowly. "I do love him. But I didn't know it until he kissed me just now."

Suddenly her sobbing was renewed as she moaned, "Why did God let this happen to me? Why did I have to fall in love with him, of all people, of all the others I could have loved, with even you, Mark, when there was no hope for either of us? Why, oh why did this have to happen?"

"I don't know, my dear," he said. "There are so many things that happen which we can't understand. But God does not expect us to understand everything. He just expects us to trust and believe in Him. Even in the face of this terrible testing, God's Word is still true. 'All things work together for good to those who love the Lord.' That is His Word and His Word never fails."

"That's hard to believe just now," she said as she dried

her eyes and sat up. "Perhaps one day I shall be able to, but not now. I just can't now.

"Won't you come in and stay with me until — afterwards?" she asked when they reached home.

"I'll come back in a little while, if you want me to, but I have an urgent call to the hospital. It came before I went to the prison, but I wanted to be with you. I'm on my way there now. As soon as I can, I'll be back."

She went inside and up to her room. She was glad that her aunt was out. She shut the door and threw herself upon the bed and tried not to think, but thoughts raced madly through her disturbed mind. She recalled all the times she had talked to Bill and what she had said to him. As she looked back, she could remember those times when the look in his eyes had surprised and vaguely disturbed her, but never in all of those brief times together had he said or even given her a hint of what he felt for her. She knew now that this may have been the reason why he had avoided her when he must have been longing to be with her and to talk to her.

Why had this happened to her, she asked herself over and over as she lay there waiting through the hours between now and the end of life for him. She had forgotten that Mark had promised to return soon. She wished that she had never been made aware of this love which was so preposterous and so unwelcome, but even so she was glad that she had granted him that one kiss. She too would remember it as long as life lasted for her.

She finally fell asleep. She did not know how long she had been asleep when she was wakened by a knock on the door. It was Susan, telling her that there was someone on the phone asking for her.

"Tell them to call back later. I can't come now," she told her.

She couldn't talk to anyone now. She couldn't pretend to be interested in trivial conversation when her heart was so torn with grief.

"But Miss Meredith, it's Mr. Mark," Susan said.

She remembered then that Mark had never come. Perhaps he was phoning to tell her why he had not come. She rose wearily from the bed and followed Susan downstairs. She glanced at the clock in the hallway and her heart seemed to suddenly stop beating. It was all over. She had slept through that terrible hour. Mark was on the phone to try to comfort her. But there was no comfort for her now! It was over. Bill was gone! She picked up the receiver, then let it fall, while she dropped upon the couch nearby and began to sob again, uncontrollably.

Susan bent over her trying to find out what the trouble was and to comfort her while Mark's voice at the other end of the line called again and again, but his call went unheeded by Meredith and the much worried Susan.

CHAPTER **24**

BILL GORDON WAITED AS IF FROZEN into immobility as the slow steps came down the corridor. He knew what was coming. Someone would come in and slit the leg of his trousers so that the electrodes could be attached to his bare leg, then he would be led down to the death chamber where his life would be burned out in one bolt of high-powered current. There would be one convulsive movement and a second or two of terrible agony, then darkness and then — what?

He knew every detail up to the end for he had read it many times and had pitied those who had gone out through that death chamber. Now it was his turn.

After death, what then? How he longed to know the answer as he waited for those steps to draw nearer and to hear the door unlocked for the man to enter. Meredith had tried to tell him but he had refused to believe. Now it was too late. Soon he would know the answer. If eternity was what she said it was, it would be far worse, ten thousand times worse, than what he was about to face.

His soul grew sick within him and fear seized him so strongly that he had difficulty in controlling this mounting terror. He did not want to go to his death a trembling coward, but an overpowering weakness robbed him of his frozen immobility and he was compelled to sit on the side of the bunk while he waited.

The warden had asked him if he would like the ministry of some spiritual adviser but he had refused it. He was sorry now that he had refused. He remembered Mark and wished that he might have a chance to talk with him, but now it was too late. A wave of nausea swept over him and he felt weak and ill, but when the door opened he managed to get to his feet and stand quietly while the knife ripped open his trouser leg.

The march down the corridor was not long, but to him it seemed miles, for he was fighting against almost overpowering weakness. He wanted to reach that chair and sit down before he fell. He must not let those witnesses know how near the breaking point he was.

At last they reached the door and it was opened quietly. He saw the sheriff and the legal witnesses and the other two standing by. One must be the coroner and the other must be the physician required by law. He glanced around looking for Terry, for he knew that Terry must be there. There was no sign of him and there was a whispered conversation between the sheriff and one of the other men. Bill was led to the chair and the electrodes were place in contact with his flesh which was now as cold and clammy as it would be a little while later when death had actually come.

Just then Terry came in. His face was ashen and his eyes refused to meet Bill's as he came forward to see that everything was as it should be. He examined the electrodes and then the switchboard before he came over to put the black cap on which would blot out sight forever from the condemned man.

Bill looked him squarely in the eye and Terry quailed visibly. His hand shook so that he could scarcely manage to put the cap on. At last everything was ready. Nothing remained but the pulling of the switch. Terry walked like an automaton toward the large lever at the switch box and raised his hand to pull the switch. Those who stood waiting were as immovable as statues. They were to see a man's life being snapped out in a moment. It was a horrible thing to witness. Some of them had seen death in battle and they had sat beside friends or loved ones while they breathed their last, but this was different, horribly different. Here was a man, young, strong, handsome and healthy, who would in a few moments, after one convulsive surge, be left a lifeless corpse.

Terry's hand reached toward the switch, then suddenly he withdrew it and backed away from it.

"I can't do it!" he screamed hysterically. "I can't do it! I can't do it!"

While the astonished witnesses and the sheriff stared at him, he fell to the floor and rocked back and forth sobbing convulsively.

There was no precedent for this unusual interruption and the sheriff didn't know what to do about it. Bill had slumped forward as if he were already dead. There was no one else commissioned to do the deed and the sheriff knew full well that he would never take it upon himself to pull that switch. They all seemed in a state of shock and no one said a word. They just stood there looking down at Terry who was moaning as if he were in physical pain.

They were startled by the loud pounding on the door and a voice shouting in excited tones, "Open up! Open up! Stop the execution! There is new evidence. Open the door!"

The sheriff was too dazed to obey the loud cries at first, but as they continued, he opened the door and admitted the excited warden. The warden looked at the body of Bill slumped forward in the chair and he uttered a groan.

"Oh! Am I too late?" he cried. "God help me! Am I too late?"

"No," the sheriff told him. "Not unless the prisoner died of shock. The switch was never pulled."

Mr. Harris and the sheriff went over to Bill and pulled off the cap. Bill raised his head weakly and looked at them through dazed eyes.

"Thank God! Thank God!" the warden murmured as he removed the electrodes. "I was afraid I was too late."

"What happened?" Bill asked dazedly.

"Tony has confessed that he killed Sam," the warden told him. "Let's get out of here, boy. This has been a terrible ordeal for you."

Bill did not even look at Terry as they left the room. He was too dazed to think of anything but that he was still alive and that soon he could lie down and rest.

When Mark received the call from the hospital he had no idea who it was who wanted to see him and he was not aware that the patient was so dangerously ill. As he entered the hospital and made his way to the ward where the patient was, little did he know what would be the outcome of that visit. As soon as he saw the patient, he recognized Tony. The nurse told him as they were going down the hall that the patient was dying and when Mark saw him he knew that death was near.

"I'm sorry I didn't get here sooner," Mark said as he stood by the bed.

"I was afraid I'd go before you got here," the dying man gasped weakly. "I've got something to tell you."

Mark sat down and took the man's hand in his and said, "Tell me what it is. I want to help you if I can."

The nurse and an intern stood by while Tony gasped out his story, stopping frequently while he struggled for breath. He confessed that he had killed Sam. He said he was glad when he learned that Bill was charged with the crime. He confessed how he had hated Bill for betraying their plot to the warden and both he and Sam had been waiting to get him for what he had done. In the meantime he and Sam had become bitter enemies and Sam had threatened to get him.

Then he had come to the meeting that afternoon. He was nervous and had nothing to do and it would be a chance to get out of his cell for a while. He was curious to know what went on in that meeting. Conviction had come upon him and he saw himself as a sinner awaiting sure punishment at the hands of God even if he escaped the law. He had wanted to talk with Mark and try to gain the peace which Mark had spoken of for those who believed, but he knew that this would compel him to confess his crime and he was afraid. Then retribution had come suddenly and relentlessly by the hemorrhage in his lung. He had had an arrested case of tuberculosis before he had been put in prison.

"God sure is making me pay for my sin," he gasped. "I was such a coward that I wouldn't confess because I was afraid to die. Now I'm dying anyway." A long pause followed while he struggled for breath and strength to continue. "I guess He didn't want Bill to pay for my crime. I guess He was right." His lips twisted in a faint smile. "Like you said, God is just. I escaped man's law, but I can't escape God's law."

Mark took out a pad and hastily wrote a few words on it.

"Can you sign this, Tony?" he asked. "It's your confession. Bill is due to die in just a little while."

"Sure I'll sign," Tony agreed. "I didn't know it was so soon."

Mark held the pad for him and held his hand while he signed his name. Then he turned to the nurse and intern.

"Sign yours," he said. "And please hurry. There is not much time to lose."

They signed the paper and Mark was about to leave when he looked again at Tony. The man's eyes were pleading and he asked in a voice scarcely above a whisper, "You gonna leave me now like this? I ain't ready to meet God. What can I do? Can't you help me?"

Mark was eager to be on his way to the prison, but he could not leave the dying man without trying to show him the way of salvation. He asked the intern if he could find someone to take the confession to the prison and to phone the warden that it was on its way. The intern said he would do it himself.

Mark turned back to Tony and talked to him, giving him the plan of salvation as simply as he could, but he was not sure that the man understood. He was already drifting into a coma and his mind was not too clear. Mark knelt by the bed and prayed, but while he was praying, the soul of Tony went out into eternity, whether to stand judgment for sin at the final judgment or to enter eternal life, Mark could not tell. It was a slim chance for one who had spent a life of crime with a soul soiled by hatred and the desire for revenge.

Mr. Harris was in the office waiting for the end of the execution. His soul was sick within him, for he felt that this was murder, not justice. He had hoped against hope that Terry would confess the truth, and save Bill, but he knew what this would mean for Terry and he knew how weak Terry was. His heart ached for Terry, who had brought this terrible thing upon himself. Terry had come into the office after he had inspected the equipment in the death chamber before time for the execution, for it was required that he should make his report. Neither of them said a word beyond what was necessary, but Mr. Harris' eyes held Terry's wavering gaze. Terry left as soon as he had given his report and Mr. Harris bowed his head while he waited for word that the ordeal was over and the law had been fulfilled.

He glanced at the clock presently and knew that in just a matter of minutes Bill would be dead. Then the telephone rang insistently. He was in no mood to talk to anyone and he thought at first that he would let it ring, but when it continued he took off the receiver and answered. What he heard electrified him into action. The voice at the other end of the wire said that Tony had confessed and that someone was on his way with the signed confession.

While the voice was still talking, the warden was ringing his bell for emergency. A guard rushed into the room thinking that perhaps there was an escape, but the warden sent him flying down the corridor with the news that Bill was innocent.

"God grant that we are not too late," he breathed as the young fellow with swifter feet than he raced toward the death chamber. He followed as fast as he could.

When Terry finally recovered himself enough to leave the death chamber he went to the warden's office. He knew that he would have to face his uncle sooner or later and he might as well get it over with now. His uncle greeted him with grave face and accusing eyes.

"Why did you do this, Terry?" he asked. "Why did you let your hatred lead you into this?"

"I thought he was guilty," Terry said as he tried to regain his self-confidence.

"But you lied to send a man to his death. You didn't see him kill Sam."

"No," Terry admitted, "but I thought he did. He was there with that knife in his hand and there was no one else nearby. He had already killed one man and he knew that Sam was after him. This would be a good way to get Sam out of the way."

"That will be poor defense if you are brought to trial for perjury," the warden said as he shook his head sadly. "I feel sorry for you, Terry, for you've thrown your life away just for hatred and you have no excuse to offer but your hypocritical plea of justice."

"Do you think I will be brought to trial for perjury?" Terry asked fearfully.

"Do you think you shouldn't be?" his uncle responded gravely. "If the truth had come out too late to save Bill, you should be tried for murder. Go home and think it over and thank God that you don't have that crime to answer for. You'll have to answer to Him for the intent to commit that crime, even though it was never actually committed. Remember that in your heart you had already committed it."

Terry looked at his uncle as horror slowly filled his eyes.

"I never thought of it that way," he said, then he turned and left the room.

He knew that his career as a lawyer was most probably finished and that he had indeed wrecked his life just as his uncle had said. Too late he remembered some of the things Meredith had told him while he basked in his self-righteousness and listened with smug indifference and unbelief. He wished that he could go to her and have her talk to him once more and help him to gain the peace of mind and heart which he knew he would need in the future which now seemed dark indeed.

CHAPTER 25

WHEN MEREDITH COULD CONTROL HER SOBS she took up the receiver again, but there was no answer and she hung up. It didn't matter. Bill was dead. Mark could say nothing that would help. She would have to battle with her grief alone. She was not alone, though. She knew that. She had known the comforting presence of God after Granny's death. She could rely on this same comfort now.

She rose and went up the stairs again.

"If Aunt Mary asks for me, tell her that I'm not feeling well and that I want to rest," she told Susan.

Presently she heard a car stop and then the ringing of the bell and then Mark's voice asking for her. She went down to see him, though she did not feel like talking to him.

"I tried to talk to you on the phone but I could hear you crying and then I hung up and came on over," he said.

"Thanks," she said dully.

"I have wonderful news for you," he said. "That's why I called you, but I'd much rather give it to you in person. Don't look so grief-stricken. Bill is still alive. Tony confessed that he killed Sam."

Her face went white and she swayed as if she was about to faint then she said in awed tones, "Then a miracle did happen!"

Mark explained briefly what had happened. He had gone to the prison as soon as he left the hospital and by that time Bill had been taken back to his cell. He had talked with the warden and had then tried to phone her. When he could not get her to answer, he had come over as fast as he could.

"Do you think I could see Bill?" she asked.

"I'm sure you can," he told her. "I don't think they could refuse you after what has happened. Let's go. I'll take you."

They were both silent as they drove along the old road which held so many memories for her, but as they neared the prison Meredith broke the silence.

"I feel so ashamed to think that I was almost rebellious against God for all that had happened. I shall have to ask for forgiveness for doubting His Word. I'm so sorry for the way I felt."

"There is a verse which has been of comfort to me many times when I've felt that I have failed God," he said. "It is in Psalm thirty-seven, verses twenty-three and twenty-four. 'The steps of a good man are ordered by the Lord. Though he fall he shall not be utterly cast down, for the Lord upholdeth him with His hand.' Another verse says, 'He knoweth our frame, He remembereth that we are dust.' I'm sure that God knows and understands."

"Thank you for reminding me of that verse." She gave him a smile. "My faithful friend! What a comfort you always are!"

The warden gave Meredith permission to visit Bill and had him brought into the room adjoining his office so that they might be alone. Bill's face still bore the marks of the strain but he greeted her with a smile.

For a moment there was an awkward silence. Both were thinking of the last time they had met and what he had said and what had happened then.

"I don't have to tell you how glad I am that you are still alive," she said. "God really worked a miracle. You'll have to admit that. Otherwise it could never have happened like it did. People would call it all just coincidence, but I know that it was God."

He nodded assent. "I've been such a stubborn, rebellious doubter," he said gravely. "When I was in that chair with that cap over my head and waiting for that current to pass through my body, I knew what an utter fool I had been. I needed assurance then of what I would face after death and I had nothing but fear and horror. I was a coward, afraid to face eternity, for I knew in that moment that what you had told me was true. Eternity would be a long time and there was no hope for me.''

"But there is hope now," she assured him with a bright smile, even though her eyes were brimming with tears. "Perhaps God knew that it would take even this to make you believe that there was no hope or peace except in Him."

"I wonder if He would forgive me now when I have been so bitter toward Him, when I even refused to believe that there was a God.''

"I know He will, if you'll only ask Him," she assured him. "Would you let Mark talk to you? I'm sure he can help you. He'll pray with you if you want him to and I know that if you will only ask, God will forgive you and give you eternal life.''

She felt that she couldn't talk to him with the same freedom with which she had talked before. The memory of that kiss and of what he had confessed to her and the knowledge of her own love for him made her too self-conscious. Perhaps he might agree to do what she asked, just because she asked it and she did not want that. When he yielded to God, it must be with the knowledge of his need and not an act that might be just to please her.

"Yes, I would like to talk to him," he said.

"I'll tell him that you want to see him," she said as she rose to leave. "I'll see you again soon."

"Wait," he said. "There's something I must say before you go. I want you to forget what I told you the last time we met. Just forget that I ever said what I did. Don't think I don't appreciate what you did. But now things are different. Forget it, please. Come to see me as often as you wish, but just as if that had never happened."

"Of course, if that's the way you want it," she replied and then went out to get Mark.

She thought she understood why he had said that, but

her heart was heavy. She thought that Bill realized that, though he had been exonerated from this crime, there still remained the old one. He was still a condemned murderer and as such he had no right to love her. He had said as much when he had asked for that kiss. But that could not alter the fact that she loved him and while she waited for Mark, she still wondered why this happened to her. Why couldn't she have loved Mark or one of the boys back home? Why did it have to be someone under a life sentence with no hope of freedom?

When at last Mark came out his face was radiant and she knew that finally the barrier of stubborn unbelief had been broken and that Bill had yielded his life into God's keeping. No matter what happened in the future, he would have peace in his heart and assurance of what lay beyond this life.

On their way home Meredith told Mark what had been on her mind while she had been waiting for him.

"Mark, I'm determined to look into the case against Bill. I believe he told me the truth about that crime he has been convicted for. How can I go about it? You know something about law. Will you help me?"

"You know that I will," he replied. "I've been thinking about that myself because while I talked to Bill, after we had prayed together, he declared that he was innocent of that crime. That was the one thing which had made him so bitter and he still couldn't understand why it had happened to him."

"Then I'm sure that this is in the will of God, if we were both thinking about it," she said. "I believe that we'll find the evidence that we need to reopen the case."

"First, we'll have to get all the facts from Bill and then I'll have to see if I can examine the records of the case on file at the court house. We may not get anywhere, but we can at least try."

"I know that if he is innocent, God will help us to prove it," she maintained.

He smiled at her tenderly as he remarked, "Your faith has been revived and I'm glad for you that it has."

"I hope and pray that it will never be so weak again," she said.

"I hope it will never be tested so severely again," he replied.

His smile was encouraging but in his heart there was a great ache. He was asking the same question that she had asked. Why did it have to be Bill? Why couldn't it have been himself?

CHAPTER 26

MARK BEGAN HIS INVESTIGATION of Bill Gordon's case at once. He had a talk with Bill and then he examined the records of the case. Neither gave him much additional information from what he and Meredith already knew.

Bill told him that both he and Fred, who worked with him at the bank, knew that there were certain funds in the vault which were not disturbed in the regular course of the daily business. It was a reserve which was not checked until the bank examiner made his rounds.

Bill was due to leave in two days on his vacation. He was arrested at the bus station. At the jail the police showed him the letter that Fred had written, telling them that he had seen Bill robbing the vault and that Bill had discovered him watching. Fred wrote that Bill had threatened him and that he feared for his life. When Fred failed to appear at the bank the next day, the police went to his room. The room was in disorder and gave evidence that there had been a struggle. There was blood on the floor. Though Bill protested his innocence, he was held while a search was made for Fred's body, or for Fred if he was still alive. When they could find neither, Bill was about to be released when two boys reported finding a body in the creek where they had gone to fish.

Though the body was clothed with Fred's suit and the wallet in his pocket held papers which, though water-soaked, were legible enough to prove that they belonged to Fred, the man's head had been crushed so badly and the body was so decomposed and partially eaten, that it could not be identified to the satisfaction of the coroner and others who examined the body, as that of Fred Barker.

Bill maintained his innocence, but the evidence was clear in the minds of the jurors that he was guilty. Because the body could not be positively identified, he was not given the death sentence.

Meredith did not receive much encouragement either from her uncle or from Mr. Stone, a lawyer friend of his who had been at the trial, but she would not give up hope.

"Suppose we visit the scene of the crime," she suggested to Mark after they had spent days and had gotten nowhere. "Isn't that what they always do in murder mysteries?"

"It can't hurt, even if we don't find anything," Mark agreed. "We'll see if we can find those two boys who found that body and get them to show us the exact spot where they found it."

It took them some time to find the names of the boys from old newspaper files and then they had the task of locating them, for they lived outside of town and there was no address in the newspaper accounts.

Finally they located one of the boys and he agreed to lead them to the place where he and his friend had found the body. The youngster felt his importance when they told him that they were looking for clues to the murder and he was much excited over the adventure.

His dog, a mongrel whom the boy proudly called a blood hound, just to make it more realistic, bounded along ahead of them, running in and out of the undergrowth beside the path.

"Maybe Touser will get the scent of the murderer and lead us to him," the boy said. "He's good at spotting rabbits and squirrels."

"It's not the murderer we're looking for, Bobbie," Mark said while Meredith laughed at the boy's remark. "We're looking for clues."

"I'll bet Touser could find a clue, if we only knew what kind we wanted him to look for," Bobbie insisted.

Much to their amazement and to the delight of the boy,

Touser did just that. While Meredith and Mark searched for some time and then stood looking rather dejectedly down at the slowly moving waters of the muddy creek, Touser began to bark vociferously as he jumped up and down before a hole in the trunk of a tree nearby.

"I guess he's treed a squirrel," Bobbie said as he went over to see what the dog had found. As he approached, Touser became braver and stood on his hind legs while he put one paw into the hole, trying to drag out whatever was in there.

Bobbie got a stick and poked it into the hole. A frightened squirrel came out and climbed frantically out of reach. But the stick had touched something soft down at the bottom of the hole.

"It's a squirrel nest," Bobbie exclaimed and put his hand inside, hoping to find a litter of baby squirrels. Instead he felt a bundle of rags.

"There's something down in there," he said, just a little frightened, as Mark and Meredith came over to investigate.

Mark reached in and drew out a ragged pair of trousers, then an old coat and a more ragged shirt. He stared at the garments, dirty and almost falling apart as he handled them, then he looked at Meredith with eyes that were bright with excitement.

"I think we've found what we were looking for," he said.

His hand touched something as he began to examine the rotting clothing and he pulled out a small wallet in a plastic case. He opened it while Meredith stood breathless beside him. The wallet contained a social security card.

"What is it?" Bobbie asked, wide-eyed with excitement.

"It may be just the evidence we need to get a man out of prison," Mark told him. "Touser is better than a blood hound. He may be the greatest dog hero this town has ever known."

They went back to town with their find and Mark showed it to Mr. Stone, Mr. Barton's lawyer friend.

After what seemed ages, the social security card was

finally checked. It belonged to a man who had been missing from home for three years. He had wandered away after a spell of illness. His wife thought he had committed suicide, but the body was never found. She identified the clothing as that her husband had worn the day he disappeared.

"The body found in the creek must have been this man," Mr. Stone said. "Whether Fred Barker killed him or whether he was already dead, he used the body to throw suspicion from himself and fasten a murder charge against Bill. The body wasn't weighted too heavily. He must have figured that it would come to the surface before too long and then they would stop looking for him. He would be free to spend the money then. It was a clever crime, but it proved once more that there is no perfect crime."

"Then Bill will be exonerated and given his freedom," Meredith cried. "How wonderful that will be!"

"Not so fast," Mr. Stone warned. "This is not sufficient proof, only supposition. We've got to find Fred."

"We'll never do that," Meredith sighed, disheartened once more.

"Don't say that," Mark told her. "Where is your faith? Don't let it fail you again."

She gave him a smile. "I'll try not."

Mr. Stone went to the district attorney and told him what had been discovered, then he went to the bank and had them put out another list of serial numbers of the stolen bills. They were all in large denominations and could be more readily checked than smaller bills. After that they could do nothing but wait and hope and pray. It was useless to try to search for the missing Barker, for he might have left the country, though Mr. Stone said he did not believe the fellow had left.

Since Bill was in prison for his murder, there would be small chance of anyone wanting to find him. Since he had no near relatives, no one would be interested in his disappearance. Very likely Barker figured, according to Mr. Stone, that since Bill had been convicted, those connected with the case would believe that Bill had stolen the money and they would not be on the lookout for it. Mr. Stone advised against posting rewards for information leading to Fred's arrest, for that would frighten him so that he would be afraid to spend the money.

While she waited and prayed and tried to hope, Meredith went about her activities in the church and in the prison services. She was pleased to see Bill at the services and it gave her joy to observe the change in him. The hard bitterness had disappeared and there was peace in the deep gray eyes and an interest in the messages which Mark gave so ably. She could see that there was hope now where there had been despair and hopelessness and she prayed earnestly that this hope might soon be realized.

Finally, after several months of impatient waiting, when they had begun to wonder if they would ever get any further with the case, Mr. Stone came to them with the news that officials in a bank in a distant state reported they had received one of the bills. This news gave them renewed hope, for they knew that it would be only a question of time when their waiting would be rewarded.

It was nearing Christmas when Fred Barker was finally arrested and brought back for trial. He confessed that he had found the man whose body had been discovered in the creek, not far from town. The man was dying. He had thought he would try to get the man to a hospital but while he was trying to get him in his car, the man died.

He had been trying to think of a plan to rob the bank and as he examined the man the idea came to him that he later used. The man was about his same height and build, so he had put his clothes on the dead man, then mutilated the body and sank it in the creek. The rest was easy, for Bill had complete confidence in his honesty.

The trial was soon over and Fred was sentenced to a long term in prison while Bill was exonerated and set free.

Meredith was shocked and hurt more deeply than she would admit, even to Mark, when Bill disappeared without even telling her good-by. He had thanked them when the trial was over and Meredith was waiting eagerly to see him, for she had asked him to come to see her, but he never came.

Just a few days before Christmas Mark told her that he would soon be leaving for the field. He had finally gotten a young minister to take his place at the church and he would be free to go when the board was ready to send him out.

"I shall miss you so much," Meredith said. "I will have no one when you go and I shall be lonely. First Mrs. Field and now you."

They did not mention Bill but Mark knew how hurt she was over his disappearance. He felt that Bill had been most ungrateful.

"You could go with me," he said hopefully.

"I wish I could, Mark," she replied sadly. "It would solve so many problems. But you know I can't. Just remember that I shall be praying for you constantly. You've meant much to me."

Christmas would be a sad day for her, for even if Mark was still there, he would be leaving soon and her life would indeed be lonely. Perhaps after Christmas she would make plans to go back to her old home. Memories there would be as heartbreaking as these were here, but there she would have Christian friends who would help her in her loneliness and sorrow.

Christmas dawned bright and sunshiny. The landscape was glittering with newly fallen snow, a truly white Christmas, with icicles hanging from drooping branches and from eaves in long fingers of crystal fringe.

Meredith had begged to be excused when visitors began to arrive in the early afternoon. Her aunt granted her request though she showed her disappointment. She was hurt over Meredith's indifference toward her guests. But Meredith felt that she couldn't face those chattering friends today. She wanted to be alone so she could give way to the gloom which possessed her and not have to wear a smile when she felt more like crying. The young minister had come to take Mark's place after Mark had received a telegram to report to mission headquarters immediately. He would not be here with her today when she most needed him. She wished that she had consented to go with him. Perhaps she could have grown to love him, but at least they would be together doing the work of the Lord among those who had never heard of Him.

Late that afternoon when most of the guests had gone, Susan knocked on the door and told her that there was someone to see her.

"Who is it?" Meredith asked. She didn't want to see anyone.

"He didn't give his name," Susan said. "I never saw him before, but he sure is a good-looking young man."

"Show him into the den," Meredith told her. "I'll be down in a little while."

When she opened the door he rose to meet her. She did not recognize him at first, for the light was dim and she had never seen him in anything but dungarees or prison uniform. Susan had told the truth. He was really a handsome young man and her heart skipped a beat as she looked into his eyes, for the love which she had thought he had forgotten shone there unmistakably and her love for him rushed through her with an emotion that was almost pain.

"This is a surprise," she managed to say while he stood there looking at her with eyes that glowed with a light which he did not try to conceal.

"I know you thought I was an ungrateful rat to disappear without even saying good-by or thanking you again for all you did for me," he said.

"I did think that you might have said good-by," she admitted. "Won't you sit down?"

"I think I can say what I have to say much better while I'm standing. When I've said what I came here for, you may not want me to sit. You may not want me to stay."

She waited for him to speak and he came closer.

"I went away without seeing you because I knew that if I saw you again, I would have to tell you once more how much I love you. I knew that I couldn't keep from telling you and I didn't want to do that. When I thought I was going to die it didn't matter, but afterwards it was different. To have a convict tell you of his love would never do. I felt that it would almost be an insult to you."

"But you're not in that class, really, Bill," she said. "You've been exonerated from every taint of crime. You are just someone who has been the victim of a terrible mistake."

"I realize that now. I've had time to think it over and I see it differently now. But if I had come to you then, I would have had nothing to offer you when I begged for a chance to win your love. I don't have much to offer you now, Meredith, but I do have a good job and the chance for a better one in the future."

He paused for a moment while she waited breathless for him to continue.

"I tried to stay away, for I know that there could be no reason for me to hope that you could ever care for me. You've known me only as a prisoner and a rebellious, bitter one who was not halfway decent at times. But I couldn't stay away. I love you so much, Meredith. Would you give me the chance to win your love, or is there someone else? I've been afraid that it might be Mark."

She smiled into his anxious, pleading eyes.

"There is no one else, Bill. Only you."

He stared at her a moment in speechless surprise, too amazed to believe that he heard aright.

"Only me?" he achoed. "You can't mean — you don't mean — it can't be true that you love me!" he stammered.

She nodded and smiled again at his bewildered surprise.

"I didn't realize it until you kissed me there in the death cell," she said as color flooded her face. "Then I knew and only Mark knows how I suffered when I thought that would be the last time I should ever see you."

"Would you be willing to risk your life with me when I'm so unworthy?" he asked, still unable to believe what she had said.

"Yes, Bill. I'm willing to take the risk."

He held out his arms to her and she came into their embrace while their lips met and he held her close.

"God has truly worked another miracle," he murmured while he held her with his cheek against hers. "I shall spend my life trying to be worthy of you and of all that He has done for me through you."

"We shall both spend our lives trying to share with others what He has given us," she said softly with her head upon his breast. "This has turned out to be the best Christmas of them all when I thought it would be about the worst."

"With God to guide us, each one shall be more happy than the last," he murmured as he bent and kissed her again.

****

They were traveling over the old road on their way to Wayne. Meredith and her bridegroom were going back home. Bill had told her later that the job he had obtained was in the bank in Wayne. He had gone there in the hopes of getting this job, for he knew that she had longed to go back there. He had carried with him a letter from the bank president where he had been employed before the robbery, as well as other letters and he had obtained the position immediately. He was hoping, though that hope was faint, that he could bring her back there one day as his wife. Now that hope was being realized.

In spite of Meredith's preference for a quiet wedding, her aunt had insisted upon an elaborate affair. Now that it was over and she and Bill were on their way, she settled quietly in the battered little car and leaned against her husband with her head resting upon his shoulder. She had insisted upon keeping the little old car, and it did have a new battery and a new set of tires.

"I think I shall keep it always as a precious souvenir," she said when Bill suggested they should get rid of it. "It was this car that brought us together."

As they came in sight of the gray prison walls, Meredith raised her head and looked at them.

"I shall be glad if I never see that place again," she remarked.

"It was pretty terrible for me," Bill replied as he slowed down and put his arm around her. "But I shall always be glad that I was there. If I had never been there I would never have known you. This has made all the rest worth while." He drew her closer. "Even that terrible experience in the death chamber."

"It was worth it if it took that to win you for the Lord," she answered softly, as she laid her head back on his shoulder. "I wondered so often why it all had to happen. Now we both know that it was all in the plan of God for us. How wonderful He is!''

As the car picked up speed and the outlines of the prison faded in the distance, Meredith began to sing softly the chorus she had been singing on that day when she had first traveled down this road.

> He's able, He's able,
> I know He's able.
> I know my Lord is able
> To carry me through.
>
> He heals the brokenhearted,
> He sets the captive free.
> He brings the dead to life again,
> And calms the troubled sea.

''How true,'' Bill whispered as he bent down and kissed her swiftly.

With their eyes upon the road ahead they drove silently into the new life awaiting them, with the sure knowledge that God was able and that in Him there was nothing to fear.